The Riddle of the Fly and Other Stories

The Riddle of the Fly

the Fly

other stories
by
Elizabeth
Enright

Short Story Index Reprint Series

BOOKS FOR LIBRARIES PRESS

FREEPORT, NEW YORK

"The House by the River" copyright 1956
The Curtis Publishing Company

"Once in a Summer" appeared originally in *The New
Yorker*. "Apple Seed and Apple Thorn" is reprinted
by permission of *Mademoiselle*. Other stories first
appeared in *Cosmopolitan, Ladies' Home Journal,
McCall's, The Texas Quarterly, University of Kansas
City Review*, and *The Yale Review*.

STANDARD BOOK NUMBER:
8369-3494-6

LIBRARY OF CONGRESS CATALOG CARD NUMBER:
70-121538

PRINTED IN THE UNITED STATES OF AMERICA

FOR CAROL AND NICHOLAS GILLHAM

CONTENTS

The Riddle of the Fly and Other Stories

The
House
by
the
River

Mrs. Schultz's house was not exactly a house; even Curtis could see that, blinded with prejudice though he was. Actually it was better than a house, for once it had been a trailer and still had a sort of peripatetic dash, an aura of experience remembered. But it had taken root. Mr. Schultz, a year or two before his death, had propped it up on a set of stolid brick and mortar legs. "There's rats down here by the river, real feisty and careless," Mrs. Schultz explained. "Hell, bite you soon as look at you. And then you never know when one of them flash floods is going to bust in and drowned you."

Not only was the trailer tamed by these stalwart legs; it had, besides, an elbowed chimney pipe, and a porch tacked onto the front of it and a shed tacked onto the back. It had a window box out of which a few petunias reached, ravaged and seedy, and another wooden box beside the steps that contained damp earth full of night crawlers. Back where the path began, close to the highway, there was a sign stuck into the ground that said, Schultz. Bait and Fresh Fish.

Mosquitoes, dangling their legs, came up at Curtis, moaning, and he struck at them, but absently. The grass under his feet was mixed with moss, patched here and there with cow dung, and near the water stood many blood-red steeples of cardinal flowers and cerulean steeples of lobelia. On the little bitten-in white beaches there was always something to find:

clam shells open and veiled with flies, old turtles locked in a stony noonday trance.

The smell was of river water and cows and broken stems, and Curtis loved this smell; he loved this place, and not only because it was forbidden. As he approached the trailer-house he felt both interested and at peace, the way one ought to feel on coming home. All around it grew the tall somber river trees, willows and box elders, sloping over it and dappling the roof with sunshine. Mrs. Schultz's radio, turned low, was the first real sound he heard (he no longer paid attention to the purling water or the ratcheting of kingfishers and cicadas), and as he came closer he could distinguish the words that were coming from it, uttered in the overemphatic tones of a radio actress: "You don't know what you're *doing* to him, Muriel, you don't know what you're *doing* to him. . . ." Curtis smiled faintly. Mrs. Schultz wouldn't be listening to that. She just turned the radio on and let it wander all day long. She liked a background of conversation, but the only time she really listened was during a ball game.

Shifting his fishing rod Curtis stepped up to the door and knocked confidently.

"Why, come in, Curtis, come right in!" cried Mrs. Schultz with pleasure. "I'm sure glad to have your company. I gathered a load of them blackberries yesterday. Got started and I couldn't *stop*. Jesus. You know how it is, you keep on and on as if pretty soon you'd find a blackberry that was better than a blackberry. I don't know. Worth money or something. And of course you never do; you wind up tore and scratched and sweaty with such a load of berries that you have to make jam. Here, try some; I'll put some on a saucer for you."

Curtis took the saucer with its auriole of flies and dipped a spoon into the hot sweet ink. "M-m, swell," he said politely.

When he had first known her, summers ago, Mrs. Schultz had often given him a little jar of this or that—jelly or pickles—to take home to his grandmother. Afterward, each time, she would ask, "Well, how'd she like it? Did she like it? Did she say it was good?" And Curtis would willingly trim up the reports of his grandmother's enthusiasm. Later he had not known how to refuse these gifts and had either had to eat them himself on the way home or to hide them in the hazel bushes for the ants to feast on. After a while when she noticed a vagueness in Curtis's replies to her questions and that he seldom brought a spontaneous message of thanks (for he was good at evasive action but not yet expert at outright lying) Mrs. Schultz stopped giving him presents to take home, but she never spoke of this, never embarrassed him by seeming to mind or wonder. In fact she had never made him feel anything but comfortable as long as he had known her.

The room smelled of hot jam and fox fur and human activity. It was a handy place, Curtis thought, everything right in reach: canned goods and clothing and pots and dishes and fishing tackle. Two clocks ticked in counterpoint on the same shelf beside many photographs and a calendar picture of an Indian maiden with an exposed breast. Mrs. Schultz's waders, which had been her husband's, stood lopped over in a corner under a hanging canopy of coats, aprons, and sweaters; and beyond the mended screen door to the porch a fox on a tether trotted to and fro with sidewise turns, his black legs stiff as branches and his tail trailing. His name was Scooter and Mr. Schultz had found him as a cub and raised him. Yet he could not really be called a pet; there was a quality about him, nervous and coldhearted, that had nothing to do with people.

Opposite the porch, at the end of the room, a brown flowered curtain hid the double bed with its two timeworn hollows, the largest of which had belonged to Mr. Schultz.

"I never lay in it, it's funny," Mrs. Schultz would say. "Even with him gone. I'm used to just my own place in that bed. I guess *so*. Forty-three years' training is something you don't get over overnight."

Barefoot, wearing a mechanic's coverall, she moved skillfully about the crowded room, swerving her head to avoid the querulous flypaper curls that hung from the ceiling, and neatly missing the corners of the furniture.

One thing that took up a lot of space in the room was Mr.

Schultz's chair. It, like the bed, bore the impress of his material magnitude. Curtis remembered him sitting there, huge in his overalls, the artificial leg straight out before him. Whenever he moved there was a creaking; a concealed leathery adjustment that brought to mind vague fantasies of the far West, of harness and Mexican saddles, dusty trails, and the hot, uncomplaining fortitude of heroes. Mr. Schultz had had a big beef-colored face and a voice all worn away with drink and shouting. He rasped in a villain's whisper, and when he laughed, as he often did, it was with a sort of silent volcanic seizure, while his face darkened to blue, and his three gold teeth, all in a row, blinked like the brass in an orchestra.

Curtis had loved Mr. Schultz. His death had come as one of the great shocks of his life.

This year he had paid his first visit to the river cabin on a fine June morning, surprising Mrs. Schultz knee-deep in the river, fishing.

"Why, Curtis! Why, hello! My God, you sure have sprouted over the winter! Four inches, I'll bet. Well, now, come on over to the cabin and have a Coke. It's just me now, you know, Curtis. Bill—Mr. Schultz—passed away in January."

"Gee, no, I didn't know," Curtis said. "Gee," he added, unable to think of anything else to say. He felt as if he had been kicked, hard, in the stomach.

"Heart," said Mrs. Schultz, reeling in her line. "Fish all gone somewheres else today anyway. Yes, it was his heart. One minute he was sitting there listening to Stan Lomax before supper, and next thing he looked up at me and said my name: 'Fern'—kind of startled. And then he just keeled over dead, and there wasn't a thing I could do."

"Gee," Curtis said.

"Yes. Well, it comes to all of us. It's hard. I miss him, Curtis. Sometimes I miss him so I can't hardly stand it, but I know good and well I haven't seen the last of him."

That was a surprise. Curtis had not expected her to be religious or superstitious. He followed her to the cabin in

silence, death having come near enough to daze him, and sat
without speaking as she poured his glass of Coke.

"Okay, buck up, owl-eyes," Mrs. Schultz said, raising her
beer glass in a gesture of greeting. "He was a great fellow, and
he wouldn't like for you to look like that, as if he's changed
to something—I don't know—scary or something. He didn't
do anything so unusual or queer. Hell, he just *died*, that's all.
Anyone can do it. Everyone *does* do it."

"It's just— I have to get used to it," Curtis said. "I never
think of anybody dying. I mean nobody I know ever does. My
father and mother did, but I was a baby; I didn't know them.
And then you read about it in papers and all, all those people
getting killed in wars and accidents, but I never know them,
either. It's just when it's somebody you *know*, like this."

"I suppose," Mrs. Schultz agreed. She looked at her glass
and turned it in her hand. "Say. I just thought. How'd you
like to have that rod of his? That English fly? He'd like for
you to have it and it never did suit me. Too souple. You could
keep it here, if you like," she added, with her effortless tact.
"How about it? Want it?"

"Man!" said Curtis.

Death, with all the pain it dealt the living, seemed nonethe-
less a little disciplined, a little trimmed of its most cruel magic,
by Mrs. Schultz's attitude. The fly rod was a beauty, too.

The jam, garnet colored, gleamed in assorted jars and
tumblers on the window sill. Mrs. Schultz wiped her red-dyed
hands on a cloth over the sink and sighed deeply.

"That's over for a year, thank God. Let's you and me get
out of here. Go fishing. Say, run and dredge me up a beer
first, will you, dear? Dredge me up a couple. I'm parched
bone-dry."

The screen door clashed behind him as he ran across the
narrow space of flattened grass to the riverbank. The beer
cans and Coke bottles were kept in an old wooden fish pen
sunk in the shadowed water near the cabin. Minnows, calico
colored, swam in and out amongst the leaning towers of glass

and copper. Curtis's arms thrust into the water were green, speckled with bubbles. The minnows swerved away in an orderly design of panic.

Mrs. Schultz believed in beer the way his grandmother believed in the Republican party. Once, two years ago, when he was eleven, she had given him some to drink.

"You need to flesh up, Curtis," she had said. "Growing like you do you look kind of—I don't know. Wrang out. Pulled. Like taffy or chewn gum. You need something to slow up your blood so it can thicken and strenthen. Why, believe it or not, when I was a kid I was skinnier than you, even. They never thought they'd raise me. Tried everything. Malt, sorghum on my mush, arn in my milk; everything. And then we knew an old woman, an old German woman, and she says give her *beer*. So they done it. They gave me beer. Well, seemed like I just had to gag it down I hated it so at first, but it wasn't long before I got the taste, and when I got it I had it for life. I guess *so*." Mrs. Schultz laughed. "And it made me flesh up fine, and you know what else? It improved my disposition! Before that I was inclined to be real mopy and feisty."

"*My* disposition isn't very good," said Curtis in some surprise, never having considered this before.

"Well, take my advice and try beer," said Mrs. Schultz. "It's pro'bly just the age you're at, but a can couldn't hurt. Here, try it."

He had not liked the beer but drank it anyway, and the resultant irresponsible mood it invoked when he got home, as well as the smell of it on his breath, were among the reasons why he was forbidden the company of the Schultzes. Another was his faithful imitation of Mr. Schultz's speech.

"There's the biggest son-of-a-bitch catfish you ever seen, down to Coover's Slough," he had remarked to his grandmother one evening at dinner, and she had taken it hard.

But those things had happened in the old unguarded days. He knew better now. Kids *have* to lie if they're going to grow up comfortably, he thought. The bottles and cans he was hold-

ing made wet blots on his T-shirt, cold and pleasing against
his ribs. In the cabin Mrs. Schultz was ready. She had put on
her old straw hat; she had a cigarette in her mouth and a can
opener in her shirt pocket. Her big face was peony-red, and
the sweat ran down her cheeks in tears.

"You look kind of hot," Curtis said.

"It's just my pressure," she said. "My pressure gives me a
real high color. They tell me don't eat *salt*. Don't eat *meat*.
I don't listen to 'em. It don't bother me none, my pressure;
just sings in my ears some days, like a hornet."

They went to a little promontory where they often fished,
and settled down under the willows. In this deep tent of shade
the jewel weed grew tall and tender, and there was a smell of
mint. Beyond, to the west, the river flowed, a melting of light,
and the gnats and flies that skimmed above it were lighted
too, fringed sparks against the dark of the sandstone bluff on
the other side where the cliff swallows had their little links
of tenements and tunnels.

Soon there was a great sound of crunching and sighing, the
toneless tonk-tonk of a bell: a cow looked down at them, her
head framed in leaves, her jaw moving to a stately measure.
Her huge eyes had the bloom of plums, and she wore her bell
like a love-locket.

"All right, you seen us," said Mrs. Schultz. "Call again when
you can't stay so long."

The cow withdrew her head and turned away, walking
with a jointed, syncopated gait.

"They're set in their ways just like females always are,"
Mrs. Schultz said. "Mornings they start out from Stever's
barn, all in single file, and they work their way down to Plow
Bottom and then acrost the narrows, taking their time. Round
the time of the noon whistle they're up to them hills back
there, and then I lose track of them till three-four o'clock
when they come by here. They just walk along the same little
old paths every day and then they stop and eat and bawl and
then they walk along the same little old paths again."

Curtis looked at his friend appreciatively. She was sitting

with her coverall cuffs rolled up and her feet in the water. The thing about her was that though she was a woman she did not worry about being a woman; she did not fuss or peek into mirrors or say "my hair is a sight." And though she was old she never seemed to worry about her age or the way somebody her age was supposed to act. If she wanted to fish she fished, if she wanted to go barefoot she went barefoot; she used her language as it came, and scratched her bites heartily, and knew as much about baseball as a boy. Curtis's grandmother was always writing letters to newspapers; she gardened with gloves on and reread novels by a man named John Galsworthy. Sometimes she would say that the weather or the state of the world or of her arthritis was "simply H, E, double L!" and after this she would laugh a little self-indulgent laugh with her cheeks pleating daintily and all her pretty pale-blue teeth showing. Nobody ever forgot that she was old or clean or a lady.

Mrs. Schultz reached for the beer can set in the water beside her feet and took a good drink. "Hell, where's the fish?" she said. "Well, I don't care though. This is good enough for me; them damn berries kept me busy as a bee in a tar bucket. My feet are all swole."

"I don't care either," said Curtis. He felt very calm and comfortable.

"Oh, this river," Mrs. Schultz said. "I don't know what I'd do without it. I take a swim first thing, mornings. It's real pretty then, and no one's around and sometimes there's, you know, a mist on the water and it's red because the sun's just up, and maybe a bunch of ducks or a heron will fly out of it, the mist, all of a sudden as if they'd just that second been made. It makes me feel pretty good usually and, Jesus, I *need* something to make me feel good. Sometimes the gang don't clear out of my place till near three in the morning."

Curtis knew about the gang—men, mostly, old friends of Mr. Schultz's, who still kept coming even after he was dead: Adey Shaughnessy, and Mr. Kriegholz, and the bearded Frantz brothers from up on Burned Hill. They liked to play cards and drink and talk, and Mrs. Schultz enjoyed those things too, and loved company.

"After they go you know what I do, Curtis? No matter what time it is? I come down to the river and walk along to that old bench where Mr. Schultz used to clean fish and cut the bait, and then I talk to him."

"You talk to Mr. Schultz?" said Curtis.

"I sure do. I tell him the news and so on. Chew the fat. Like I would do anytime. *He* don't want to be treated different."

"But he is different. Heck, he's dead."

"No, no. I don't hold with that idea: dead. I don't mean angels or any of that. I don't mean *heaven*. I mean something else."

"God, probably," Curtis said tolerantly. "Some kind of God-business or other."

"Maybe. I don't know. It's just that I don't believe it's any of it wasted, living. Not your living or my living or Mr. Schultz's. It don't just quit; it gets back into the system someways, don't ask me how. But I believe it, and so I just talk to him like I always done, so he won't feel too lonesome or different no matter what he is. And you know what else? Two times now, Curtis, I felt he was trying his best to answer me, trying his best. If only I could of listened harder or steadier or learned some new way to listen . . . sometime I'll do it, too; sometime I'll be able to hear him, and *then*, boy . . ."

A chill passed lightly over the skin of Curtis's forearms, stippling them with gooseflesh.

"Aren't you scared at all?"

"Of *him?* Of *Bill?* Would I be scared of you?"

Nevertheless it gave Curtis a strange feeling to think of Mrs. Schultz in the middle of the night talking to nobody like that, all by herself and drunk (he was old enough to know that she would probably be drunk), while the fish slopped in and out of the still river and owls called in the woods.

"Well, I don't know if it's a very practical thing to do," he said doubtfully.

"Hell, who's practical?" said Mrs. Schultz. "Say, Curtis!

You know something? I just noticed! Your voice is commencing to change!"

"I guess so. I'm thirteen."

"Is that right? Thirteen! And it don't seem like but a day since the first time you come down here to buy bait with that Calcutta surf-casting rod over your shoulder, big as a mast."

"I was dumb. When you're eight you're still dumb."

"Never again afterwards though," said Mrs. Schultz. "Honey? Run back and dredge me up another beer."

The day lengthened peacefully. The river lost its light, and the cliff swallows came out to hunt and play, their flight curving and bright. The fishing was poor; all they caught the whole afternoon was a couple of bullheads.

"Must be there's a Fish Social somewheres and they're all to it," Mrs. Schultz said. "Let's try another place real soon, how about it? I'll fix us a picnic up and we can drive over to Squaw Dam or one of the sloughs; take the day to it. Let's see—Thursday? I got to have a mess of something for Friday, sure."

"Okay," said Curtis, happily inventing explanations for his grandmother.

But on Thursday when he came down to breakfast his grandmother was wearing a hat.

"You'd better put on another shirt, dear," she said. "We're spending the day in town."

"Heck, no!"

"Oh, yes. Oh, yes," sang his grandmother implacably. "I've made an appointment for your teeth, and it will be a very good time to get you outfitted for school."

At this moment Mrs. Schultz would be constructing her good big leathery sandwiches and looking forward to the day. There was no way he could let her know. He hated his grandmother.

"You could have told me sooner, at least."

"And listened to all that grumbling beforehand?" His grandmother laughed her silvery uncomprehending laugh. "I know my Curtis, after all. Oh, yes, I know him through and through."

At half past nine that night he escaped from the house by creeping down the back stairs. As he passed the living-room windows he could see his grandmother at her desk, her head moving faintly to the movement of her writing hand. (She wrote emphatically, always, with many underlinings, and long bold strokes on the tails of the letters.)

The dark dewy grass of the orchard was clumsy with apples. The cobwebs of late summer stroked his face and clung. The night still worried him as it had when he was much younger; in itself it seemed an enemy, and his heart was thumping as he crawled under the fence and ran across the pastures downward, always downward, till he came to the dusty moon-white highway that ran parallel to the river.

At Bridge Tavern the juke box was grinding out music, and already men were heehawing at the bar. Trucks were drawn up in front, some with tow-haired babies asleep in the cab. Across the river to the left of the bridge he saw the frugal lights of Mrs. Schultz's house glimmering among leaves. When he crossed it, the bridge resounded dolefully beneath his feet; the river below was dimly polished—mysterious, like a huge empty road. At the other side he turned from the highway and made his way along the fragrant river path. The bait sign was white in the darkness; it reminded him of something. It reminded him of the cross on a soldier's grave.

The sight of the lighted cabin came as a great refreshment to his spirits, and he ran toward it calling to his friend. But there was no answer to his calling, or to his knocking when he reached the door. As he stood on the step, waiting, all he could hear was the radio, babbling low and out of focus, and when he went in he found the place disorderly, a card table, laden with stale glasses and a saucer full of butts crowding it still further. He went over to the radio and put his hand on it; it felt hot, as if it had been going for a long time, and he turned it off. Now all he could hear was the whispered dialogue of the two clocks, and the ticking of Scooter's claws on the porch floorboards.

Curtis sat down in Mr. Schultz's chair to wait. He could not remember that Mrs. Schultz had ever been away before when he had come to see her. He sat stiffly in the old sprung chair, as if the windows were posted with watchers. When he spoke to the fox his voice cracked. . . . The sound of steps on the path outside brought him to his feet, sweating with relief, and he threw open the door.

But it was only Adey Shaughnessy, tiny and thin, like an old little kid.

"Hey, Curtis."

"Hi. Where's *she?*"

"Where's she? Ain't she here? Maybe she stepped out back a minute," Adey said delicately. In a moment he raised his voice. "Fern! Hey, *Fern!*"

But there was no sound except an idle finger of wind moving among the tops of the trees.

"Well, that's funny," Adey said. "She knew I was coming tonight. And the Frantz boys, too, and Ella Gates and her niece. I'm late. Don't know where *they* are."

He came into the house. "She ain't cleaned up from last night, either. Now, that's not like Fern."

He sat down on the edge of a chair and Curtis sat on the edge of another. Adey lighted a cigarette which he held between his thumb and his first two fingers as if he were holding something else, not a cigarette.

"Her old bus is still parked in the shed. I saw it," he said, after a moment. *"She* don't go no place, anyways. Everybody comes to her."

"I know."

"And her pressure's real bad," Adey said. "She don't take no proper care of herself. I says to her, 'Fern, you oughta listen what they tell you—' "

Curtis stood up. "I think I'll go and kind of look around," he said. His stomach pained him with anxiety.

"That's not a bad idea. I'll come with you. Wait a minute now; she's got a flashlight here somewheres."

Curtis could not wait, however. He left the cabin, closing the screen door very quietly for some reason, and hurried along the moon-scattered path beside the river, which crept in silence between its banks. The air was sweet-smelling and beating with crickets. There was a glittering of fish scales on the surface of Mr. Schultz's fish-cleaning bench, and near it, as he had suspected he would, he found Mrs. Schultz.

She had fallen onto the path and lay perfectly still on her back, her eyes wide open and shining like two minnows in the moonlight. One of her arms was stretched out sideways on the ground as if it reached for something. She was still, the way rocks and stones and logs are still.

"Mr. Shaughnessy! Mr. Shaughnessy!" bawled Curtis in the shameless, shocking voice of panic.

Adey's flashlight bounded forward in erratic firefly swoops.

Afterward, when everything had been done that could be done and the car doors had slammed and the people were gone, Adey offered to drive him home.

"I guess I'll just walk," Curtis said. "My grandmother doesn't know I'm out. Thanks, though."

He waited, and then turned back along the river path.

The crickets were a long spun sound, a night-breathing all over the summer world. There was a lace of shadows, motionless, beneath each tree, and at the fish-cleaning bench all was quiet, unmarked by any event. Curtis leaned one hand on the back of the bench, and took a deep trembling breath.

"What did you say to her that made her die?" he demanded in a loud voice. And then he broke out in a sweat. What if there should be an answer?

But there was nothing except another faint stirring of wind in the trees, like the sigh of a sleeper. Of course there was no answer; Curtis was immediately sure that he had never expected an answer.

He was crying as he ran back along the river path. He

crossed the bridge at a jog trot and passed the throbbing tavern without a glance. He had no worry to spare for the dismay and anger that he might find at home, and the night itself was powerless to scare him now. Grief had made him impervious to any of the threats he knew, and in his mind a detached observer took note of this, even as he cried and stumbled through the uphill pastures.

Far down the river owls called to one another in remote, frosty voices, and on Mrs. Schultz's porch the hungry fox trotted to and fro and to and fro on his long tether.

A
Night
Watch

She opened her eyes suddenly, though no sound had wakened her. Somewhere in the enormous complex country of her sleeping mind a command of silence had roused her, a command which, echoing noiselessly, persistently, in her responses, had been terse, alarming. But now all she knew of it was this echo in her nerves; the nature of the command itself had been lost in the instant of waking.

The room was perfectly still except for a small clock stitching away, stitching away at the long night. It was a large room with windows facing on a park. The street lamp opposite laid a fan of light on the ceiling, shutter-striped, and the few cars passing also brushed lights across the ceiling and walls from time to time. The room had the calm, impersonal mystery of a well-kept house long after midnight. Its mirrors seemed asleep. There was nothing to fear and she was not afraid, but she lay there on the right side of the wide bed, tense and quiet. She lay on the right side always, from habit, though the bed had been hers to use alone for more than a year. Sometimes she still woke up and put out her arm to the cold sheet, the unindented pillow at her left side, with a feeling of shock and loss. Nothing important happens to you only once, she knew; it keeps on happening again and again in new and different ways as well as in the same old tedious ones that ding-dong throughout a life, some days faint and some days loud.

17

But now she was not feeling or thinking any of this. She was disheartened by the completeness of her waking, knowing she was faced with one of those small-hour appraisals of the future's threats and promises: pains and age; bills, loneliness, death. (Memory, tactless as a mongrel, also chooses this time to exhume old failures and bring them home for claiming: acts of dishonesty and meanness, particularly if these have been observed; stupidities, errors of judgment or justice; unconscious cruelties discovered too late, conscious cruelties admitted too late. At such a time one runs hunted among one's thoughts, searching, doubling back, turning, wretched for peace or satisfaction, but memory and promise, equally exacting, bar the way to every escape.) Homesick, she thought of her childhood sleep, profound, and lasting all night long, and she had a sudden memory of her father, years and years ago, sitting beside her crib in the dusk, singing her the Navajo songs he had learned in the West.

She snapped on the light, determined to read, but it was no use; the words ran like ants over the page and had no meaning for her. Soon she turned the light off and lay looking at the ceiling. It was three o'clock. Perhaps at five she would sleep again. At half past six the child in the next room would wake and call her, and the day would begin.

After a while she got up and went to the open window. The park was empty and silent; the street was silent. There was only one other human being in sight, a man three stories below, standing on the pavement. Cars were parked for the night along the curb, and at first she thought he was trying to unlock the door of his own car, but after a moment, seeing the careful way in which he glanced back over his shoulder, she knew that she was looking at a thief. He had got his hand through a partly open car window and was pulling something out—a robe or blanket. She saw him rub it between his fingers like a bargainer, hold it up to the light, smell it, and then, disdainfully, he stuffed it back into the car again. Not good enough. Next he reached his arm around to the inside window handle of the front door (he had very long useful arms) and wound the glass down, and then she heard a faint click as he opened the glove compartment. Pressed against the car, one arm inside it, he turned his head again quickly, to reassure himself. He saw no one. The moving cars on the avenue to the west seemed as impersonal as fish in a current. Never having watched a thief before, she was aware, beneath feelings of shock and excitement, of a certain respect, a treasonous admiration at the sight of a man doing a job skillfully, with the ease and silence of long practice. Well, good God, do something, she thought. Call out. Get the police. But for some reason she could not call out, did not dare, as if on catching sight of her the man might develop some superhuman power—spread bat wings and fly up at her, or paralyze her with the first look. And as for calling the police she knew she did not do this because she did not want to; she wanted to watch him undisturbed. And then, at that very moment, as though her thoughts had reached him, the man turned abruptly away from the car and hastened, still silent, up the street toward the avenue. It was then that she realized he had just stolen the hat on his head, for as he walked away he took it off, turned it on his hand, stroked the ribbon, examined the inside band, then returned it to his head. It seemed to fit him very well.

There was nothing to be done. A cat veered from the shadow to the light, veered back to shadow. A random wind stirred the branches of the park trees and was gone. The thief, herself, the cat, were the three live things inhabiting the quarter-hour. Live, but not alive enough; none of them (possibly the cat) utilizing a fraction of that which had been given them to use or even guessing how such use might be accomplished. The thief worked hard to steal what others had worked hard to earn, and she, if she did not steal, was guilty of other acts as base. . . . Memory and promise, which had been quieted temporarily by the sight of the thief, now returned to their accusatory dialogue and she was at their mercy again.

An image came into her mind which had occurred to her before at times like this. There was an old seashore house that they had rented many a summer in the past, a faded rackety place where the screen doors twanged, croquet balls clucked on the lawn, and the smell of roses was as firm as flesh all through the month of June.

But in the image it is January. There is no one in the house. Lattices sift the black night wind; a bitter sea torments the beaches. Vines scrape at the shingles, and inside the house is deathly cold and filled with that silence which in the end triumphs over all. Summer's noise and play and living are here shown up for what they always were: a skirling of leaves, papery, ephemeral; a short dance soon over, soon over, and now recognized to have been of little consequence while it lasted.

She found that she was shivering and not from cold alone. The image of the winter house seemed the sole truth to her, and there was no voice to deny that this was so. All around her stood the huge stone ugly city, riddled through and through with little extinguishable pulps of life, and murmuring with the vague insomniac monologue of cities at night. She leaned on the sill for a long time, inspecting this personal nadir of hers, giving it the studious attention one gives to a physical pain, as if by classifying its component parts one might understand and therefore temper it a little.

The sound that finally roused her had been going on for some time before she began to listen to it consciously. It had begun in the distance, to the west of the park, faint but insistent at first, and steadily growing louder as it came closer: a man's voice, singing. He was singing at the top of his lungs, and all by himself, too, for after a few minutes she could see him at the far end of the park, a tiny figure, strutting, solitary, shouting his song, first in the round light of one park lamp, then nearer and louder in the light of the next:

> *Vorrei, e non vorrei*
> *Mi trema un poco il cor,*
> *Felice, e ver, sarei,*
> *Ma puo burlarmi ancor . . .*

She could tell that he was drunk, on the edge of staggering, but he was happy beyond the bounds of reality. Was he in love? Or was it only that he had reached his particular zenith of alcohol? She saw that he was shabby, not young, but as he advanced proudly from one stage of light to the next he brought with him a ludicrous splendor, as though he marched adorned with lights and chimes and pennies hung from threads, a one-man parade, as determined in joy as a bridegroom. His voice had once been fine and there were shreds of beauty in it still:

> *Vorrei e non vorrei*
> *Mi trema un poco il cor . . .*

Zerlina's song over and over; that one verse as if he had invented it and was wild with pride, the way a rooster is wild with pride each morning, believing it has invented day. He was laughable and she laughed, watching him, the small man strutting away from her, and away and away, still bawling his maidenly song. And now she noticed how cold she was, shivering. Rubbing sill grit from her icy elbows, she made her way across the dim room and into bed. Soon she was warm in it; it held her softly all around, predicting sleep.

> *Vorrei e non vorrei*
> *Mi trema un poco il cor . . .*

Smiling lazily she listened to the voice, very far away by now, across the park and in some street. She wondered what would silence it in the end. Protests through opened windows? Shoes or cold water in the face? The realistic agents of the law? His joy seemed indestructible and she still heard the little voice proclaiming it as she drifted deeper and deeper into sleep.

At six-thirty her two-year-old son called to her. When she went into his room she found him standing in his crib, grasping the railing and rattling it. His straight hair stood out from his head in rays and his cheeks were chapped red. He began to jump as she came near, and when she lifted him out he felt warm and healthy and smelled of urine. She held him on her hip as she lifted the window shade and turned to look at him in the early light. Close to hers his clear gray eye observed the world, gazing calmly, as an animal gazes, still unambiguous, still undeflected by considerations of effect and reward. How would the world appear through such a lens? she wondered, and turned her head, following the direction of his serene regard, trying to imitate it.

A waning moon was still in the sky, its shadowed marks exactly the color of the sky at this moment, so that it looked as if it had been greatly used, worn through in places. High above, in light which had not yet descended, two gulls were flying, their leisured flight reminding of space and oceans. Below, the park was still in shadow, but beyond it to the south the ugly flat-topped factories and office buildings were touched with rose; they seemed to float like mesas far across a desert floor. Her child's arm tightened around her neck; he yawned aloud and she could feel the movement of his jaw against her cheek. It was infectious—she yawned too—and for the moment at least, her eye like his looked out on a fair morning world.

Once
in
a
Summer

Christy sprang up from the lunch table with a stifled sob that sounded more like a snicker. They heard her running helter-skelter up the stairs. A door slammed—just one more in a series; doors had been slamming since eight o'clock, but the others had been pushed by the east wind and not by sorrow.

Tim, her husband, who was believed to be the cause of her rout, went on eating his Golden Bantam. A yellow kernel had stuck itself to his cheek and wobbled guilelessly as he chewed, somehow emphasizing his look of guilt and stubbornness.

"What's the matter with Aunt Christy?" demanded Pammy. "Why did she rush away like that before dessert? Mother? Mother? Why did she?"

Marjorie glanced across the table at Gordon, who raised his eyebrows and lighted a cigarette: You handle it, he meant. This was often his message.

"Aunt Christy doesn't feel very well, darling. She doesn't want dessert today."

"But, heck, it's butter pecan. Mrs. Beavers told me," said Normy.

"Well, she doesn't want any butter pecan. She'll be better soon," Marjorie added encouragingly. "It's nothing very serious."

Pammy naturally did not believe this explanation (Normy did, perhaps, being only seven), and she knew that her mother

did not really expect her to believe it. It was the sort of for-
mality to which children are treated, a meaningless codicil like
"excuse me" after belching, and as such she accepted it, asking
no more questions but regarding her Uncle Tim in a way that
caused him to bite his tongue. Red with pain, he laid the
corncob down on his plate but said nothing, knowing ob-
scurely that a bitten tongue, admitted, would be more evidence
against him. At the moment he felt the whole idea had been a
mistake, anyway, this business of sharing a house for the summer. The sisters, Marjorie and Christy, were the ones who
had wanted it, and as long as their husbands had been week-
enders only, the plan had worked out well; but now with one
week of vacation behind Gordon and himself and two more
to go, Tim was not so sure. Living with new relations, no
matter how congenial, was a strain, and it still disconcerted
him to be called "Uncle Tim" by the children. Who, me?
was his reaction every time. He was not sure exactly how an
uncle was supposed to act. Wise, probably, he thought; wise
and informative. A real uncle would not cause his wife tears
—at least not in public—or suffer from hangover, or bite his
tongue. . . . At these thoughts a treasonous loud sigh escaped
him, and he felt additionally exposed by the overhead light,
an anachronistic fixture of glass, brass, and bead fringe, which
cast a glare like the light in an operating theater. Though it
was only one o'clock, the thing was turned on because of the
black weather out of doors.

The day had been hell from the beginning. They had come
home too late from the Phelpses' party the night before and all
of them (except Marjorie, who drank very little) were uncomfortable in the head. Marjorie, waking early, had heard her
sister crying in the next room; even though she was crying
carefully, she was audible, for in this house it was impossible
to keep any secret involving sound. The next thing was the
arrival of the east wind, which announced itself by knocking
over a tumbler full of toothbrushes in the bathroom and slamming four doors. Soon the shutters were stammering and
fidgeting at their hooks, and the rain was coming sturdily in

at the windows and soaking the floor matting, which would
now mildew. The bottled gas ceased to breathe shortly before
breakfast so that nothing was warm enough to be cooked
through, and they had had to eat dry cereal and milk and
cold plums. "This meal was planned for the perpetuation of
the hangover," grumbled Gordon; "to make it strong, potent,
and full-bodied. My God. No coffee. Today, no coffee." Tim
said nothing; he looked chastened and unwell. And Christy
was solicitously ignored because of her pink eyelids and wist-
fully swollen lip. In the kitchen Mrs. Beavers dropped a box
of eggs. The children whined and bickered throughout the
morning; this sort of weather always caused them to revert to
younger age levels. And added to everything else, the spaniel,
Emma, was in season. Many wet dogs assembled on the porch
to groan and plunge against the rain-trimmed door, and anyone going out had to press himself through the narrowest
possible space, fending off besiegers with his shinbone.

Now as they were finishing dessert Mrs. Beavers struck the
kitchen door open. "Mrs. McLeod, the cesspool's backing up.
All over the yard, it is." She made the announcement with a
sort of triumph. Now this! At last! The culmination!

"Oh, dear." Marjorie pushed back her chair, which scraped
shrilly. "I'll have to call that man in Teaquog. Mr. Sweet."

The children, springing to their feet, looked happy for the
first time.

Gordon and Tim remained a little longer beside the sham-
bles of the lunch table.

"Mr. Sweet" said Gordon. "If people were responsible for
their surnames you'd think he'd had an overdose of Dickens.
Or Saroyan."

"Mrs. Beavers, too," said Tim. "Only in her case I guess it
would be Galsworthy, or some one of those other English guys
that patronize the servants in their novels by giving them
those names: Bumble and Fumble and Feathers and Beavers
and so on."

"Any resemblance to Galsworthy ends with the woman's
name," Gordon said; "and you could never call her a servant,

either. You could call her Emily Post or Maria Edgeworth or someone like that, doing us a favor incognito."

Tim did not reply. Dropping cigarette ash into his ice cream, he gave another loud involuntary sigh.

"Trouble? About last night?" Gordon said.

"Oh, yes. My God, it wasn't anything but a kiss; kisses, I guess. A little necking. You know. And I was high. Nothing. The whole thing was *nothing;* and Christy will not understand it."

"Well, you've been married hardly a year. You must admit that sort of thing doesn't usually take place so soon."

"Call me precocious," said Tim sulkily.

"And then Christy's a very sensitive girl—" Sensitive! he thought to himself. That word, spoken as praise, as commendation, the way it is nowadays! What is our sensitiveness but a morbid attention to the ego, a counting over of its bruises, hourly, as if they were treasures?

"I better go up and see," said Tim.

"Good luck."

When Gordon came into the living room, Marjorie was putting down the receiver. "He's coming right over, thank goodness."

"Mr. Sweet?"

"Yes. He sounded very happy about it; on a Saturday, too. There's a man who loves his work!"

Gordon put his arms around her waist and pulled her back against him. "Do you know why I married you?"

"You tell me."

"It's because you're not sensitive."

"Well, listen, I'm not so sure I like that!"

"Yes, you do. You like it very much. You know what I see when I say that word? Sensitive, the way they mean it nowadays? I see a nice clean monkey with a face like a man's who's worried sick about money. He's sitting on a branch—out on a limb, probably—and very daintily picking the fleas off himself with those little ice-cold fingers they have. And then he eats them one by one, choicely, as if they were crumbs from the king's table."

"Well, I'd call that sort of a sensitive analogy, honey. I might even call it sort of precious."

"Oh, sure. I'm a charter member of these lousy times. I belong in the zoo, too. Let's go upstairs and have a nap."

On the stairs they passed Tim coming down, failure in his glance.

"And anyway I read someplace it's not fleas that monkeys pick off and eat like that," Marjorie said. "It's little tiny flakes of salt from the skin. All animals are supposed to need salt in their diet."

"Steady now; don't overdo it," Gordon said. "It's fine to be realistic and all that, but God pity the metaphor in the hands of a literal woman!"

"Well, my goodness, there's no satisfying you today, Gordon. *Temperament*, I'm so sick of *temperament*. First Christy in tears and now you snapping. And Tim glooming and heaving around the house. What's the matter with those two, anyway?"

"Oh, he helped himself to a little slap and tickle last night with that girl at the Phelpses'. That spoon-faced girl. Christy's taking it hard, so we're all being punished."

"Oh, dear."

"Yes, well, why on earth you and your sister thought this joint venture would be a good idea in the first place—"

"Gordon, *sh-h!*" Marjorie closed the door.

"The family nucleus has trouble enough just getting along in itself without calling in extras to add to the supply." But being forced to whisper lamed his objection considerably.

"Gordon, please stop hissing like an adder," hissed Marjorie. She went to the window and looked out at the wrecked day. The curtains smelled of wet scrim and the screen was crosshatched with cuneiform rain scrawls. She yawned aloud. Oh, the burden of afternoon and bad weather and too many people under one roof! The best thing to do is to bury oneself in sleep, but the house resounded, thumped, gabbled, and now the radio downstairs added a pulsing male voice to the accumulation of noise. It would be Gordon, the sensitive one, who fell asleep in spite of all, Marjorie knew, while she, the realist, would stay awake and chafe at her dull thoughts.

Downstairs Tim lay on the living-room couch, uncomfortably, with his head on one of the arms, his feet on the other, and the radio turned up to a healthy pitch beside him. There is always one ball park in the world that has not been rained out. Tim found the manic roars of the crowd, the passionate emphasis of the announcer, very soothing to his galled spirits. He enjoyed quarreling with the decisions. "Aw, what've you got him up for? He couldn't hit it with an oar! He couldn't hit it if it was a grapefruit!" He yawned and argued, half asleep; the children wrangled close at hand.

"It's my turn, it's my turn!"

"Drop dead, Normy, it is not! You had two turns already. I bet you even had *three!*"

"Why don't you kids go over to the Harbisons'?" suggested Tim, rousing.

"They've gone to Teaquog to the movies."

"What about the Phelps twins, then?"

"They're still in the nap-taking stage, the big babies."

"Not a bad idea. When'd you people outgrow it?"

"Oh, long ago. *I* did. Normy's still supposed to."

"They got discouraged finding me and making me every day," said Normy.

"Well, go *some*place, why don't you? Get some air. It's not raining any more; much."

In the end he succeeded in getting them out of the house, and rolled over ready for sleep, the ball game a loud lullaby for his ear. But before he got anyplace with it the children were back, bringing other children home to quarrel with. The screen door slammed constantly, and dogs kept getting in and trotting briskly about the house, looking raffish and intent, until they were collared and put out. Tim groaned and increased the volume of the radio.

. . .

Christy sat in a cackling old rocker putting polish on her nails. Because of the wet day it would take them forever to dry, but she did not care; she had time and there was nothing else to do. She could not write letters, feeling as she did, and she had read everything in the room. If she left the room to look for something new Tim might think that she was cured of grief. From time to time she sniffed reminiscently, and her cheeks still felt salty. Painting on the lacquer carefully, slowly, she silently made speeches to her husband while he listened without interrupting. The speeches took varied forms for she could not make a choice between the several methods of attack or reproach. There was the cold toneless voice, for instance: "I suppose it's better, in a way, to learn these things early in a marriage. Heavens, what a perfect fool you must have thought me," and then a little laugh. Or there was open rage: "Just who the hell do you think I am? The kind of wife who mopes in the background and warms her husband's slippers till he's ready to come home from someone else? Well, think again!" and then another kind of laugh, deep and brusque. There was renunciation: "Of course it's over. It's finished. And how beautiful I thought it was! But I am leaving on the morning—no, the evening—train." To this she added one more sentence: "Naturally I will not accept any alimony."

Suddenly Christy put the little bottle and brush back on the bureau. As she stood up, the file and scissors fell out of her lap and she left them on the floor. "How false I am, what a liar!" she whispered to herself. She saw her face in the mirror, furious, unfamiliar, and she turned away in disgust. Her spoken words seemed false as all the rest. The only real thing was this bulky boring lump of pain which she believed to be despair.

At four o'clock she decided that Tim was not coming up to try to comfort her again. The house, unstrung with noise, was finally too much to bear; she put on her raincoat and ran down the back stairs, crossing Mrs. Beavers' new-mopped floor and admitting a final dog as she went out the kitchen door.

"Forevermore!" cried Mrs. Beavers, flinging down the mop handle in a zenith of exasperation.

A truck with a round belly was gulping and grinding in the back yard; children in raincoats stood admiring it, but Christy was too preoccupied to notice. She crossed the soaked grass and turned right on the road to the beach.

As she passed the Phelps house, ugly with creosote and balconies, she thought that it, too, looked hung-over from the night before. A sodden paper napkin was stuck to the hedge; a highball glass lay tipped on the lawn; and as she passed she heard a voice inside calling, "Turn it down, turn it *down!*"

That house was the last one before the bathhouse; from here to the beach there was only a waste of bayberry and honeysuckle. Telegraph poles were the sole trees. On hot sunny days the area was a dazzle of fragrance, but today the rain had tamped it down.

Thunder had begun somewhere, and the wind had lessened. The gray torn sky hung low over her head, drifting, stingy with its rain, of which only a few scarce drops stung her brow and cheeks. The gulls creaked and whined on their shifting levels of air, and as Christy hurried she encouraged her sense of wrong. "So this is how it's going to be!" she said aloud. "So this is all it ever was!" These words succeeded in arousing a tear or two—parsimonious like the raindrops, but somehow comforting.

The bathhouse, a yellow box, lay at the end of the road. She ran up the echoing steps toward the roofless porch that faced the sea. A smell of cigarette smoke warned her, but not in time. Bay Phelps was standing there, lonely, huffy, staring at the dark foam-seamed water. She saw his leather elbow patches; the little bald spot that was taking him unawares.

He turned, and pleasure changed his face. "Christy! You're the one beautiful thing I've seen all day!"

"I haven't seen *anything* beautiful," she said unkindly. "When I looked in the mirror I saw a donkey."

"Nonsense. How's Tim feeling?"

"Rotten, thanks. We all feel rotten. And this awful day!"

"Our house is a howling wilderness. I had to get out. Katie's on the rampage. It's one of those days when she keeps telling me about my unconscious hostility to my children and what it's doing to them. Warping their lives and all that. Warping *me*. 'Traumatizing,' she calls it. I wish Freud had been born in Birmingham, England, in eighteen twenty-three. That background would have kept him in line."

"Our house is just about the same, only we've got baseball instead of Freud. I'm mad at Tim; I've acted badly. I've shown it."

"He'll forgive you."

"When will I forgive him, I wonder? I hate being like this."

As they spoke the heavy falling combers and the slow plunging thunder had been keeping up a dolorous counterpoint, and now, as if from impatience, the long-drawn-out foreplay was abandoned in favor of sudden and violent consummation. Rain opened on the world, and lightning, white and deathly, skipped across the waves.

"It's a deluge! Here, come in here!"

He pulled her into an empty cubicle. Number 22 was painted on the clapping door. The place was dim and smelled strongly of damp towels. Rain dinned on the roof, and wind ran like wolves under the loose-planked floor. A small mirror on a nail winked back its version of the lightning.

Bay had pulled down a bath towel and was blotting Christy's wet face and hair. She drew back in distaste. "But we don't know who it belongs to!"

"Oh, yes, we do. It's mine. This is the Phelpses' bathhouse."

He looked at her, smiling, tossed the towel aside, and took her in his arms. He smelled of damp tweed, his cheek was rough, and his mouth in that wet cold face was hot and skillful and determined. Completely surrounded, beard-scratched, tweed-scratched, enclosed, tasted, she thought, But where am I? Someplace far away, not here; I am certainly not taking part in this. . . . And then, even as she thought it, she found to her surprise that she was taking part; that she was suddenly ignited, and presently as greedy and reckless as he was—or not quite, for in the nick of time she pulled herself loose.

"No, let me go, let me *go!*" She cried it savagely, glad to leave him in his frustration, rumpled, and grotesque with lipstick.

The bathhouse floor drummed to her running feet. The rain was cold and dense enough to drown anybody's passion; the lightning snipped the sky with scissor slashes. As she ran, fending off thunder, she scrubbed at her face with scraps of Kleenex and tossed them stained with pink into the beach grass. She felt surprised, triumphant, and ashamed, all at the same time, and for some reason she had an impulse to laugh.

"Christy, where have you been!"

Tim stood in the road with his hair plastered down on his brow as though he had just come out of the sea. His face looked wary—prepared to renew battle if necessary but wishing for truce. She saw that he had recently been scared.

"Did you think I'd gone to drown myself?"

She leaned her head against his chest where, nearer than all other sounds, she heard the well-known beating of his heart.

"I would never do such a thing."

"Are you all right now, Chris? Do you really think you're over it?" asked Tim anxiously, as though she were a convalescent. "A-a-h, Christy. You're my one. You're my only one."

"I know that. I know that."

Happy in the rain, they walked slowly back to the house, with the awkward gait of two of unequal size whose arms are about each other. It's not just because I've gotten even, she assured herself. It's not just because I did what he did and found out about it; it's much more complex than that. But deeper down, where truth looked out with a codfish eye, she saw that this was just exactly what it had been, nothing more and nothing better. Well, never mind, she thought; use what comes to hand for mending, and if your materials are not first-class, if they're crude, makeshift, vulgar—never *mind* if they're all you have and they do the job. What they are mending may not be first-class either, but it's what I want more than anything. It's what we want.

The rain stopped about seven. Cleared of clouds, the sky was pure, the color of honey, and all twigs, railings, blades, and clotheslines were hung with honey-colored drops. The children on their bicycles skimmed off like swallows, and true swallows, also liberated, took to the evening air. Calm settled on the house; the only sound was Gordon in the pantry, getting out the ice for cocktails.

At ten o'clock Marjorie and Gordon came out to take a turn around the garden, arm in arm. The three-quarter moon stood in the sky, a face averted, and the few stars looked very large and fresh. Not far away, but seeming far, the ocean sounded appeased, monumental.

"It's like the evening after some huge battle. Austerlitz, or something," Marjorie said. "This whole day has been a struggle to survive."

"There's one of them in every summer. Winter's full of days like that, but in summer you generally don't get more than one or two."

The windows of Tim's and Christy's room were dark. Normy's were dark. Pammy's were lighted and her radio was squawking hoarsely. They could see her, lying on her side, listening, picking at old mosquito bites.

"That kid ought to be asleep."

"Oh, what difference does it make this time of year? She can make it up in the morning. . . . Oh-oh-oh—I'm dead. Look at this night! Tomorrow will be hot and wonderful again; everything will run smoothly. I wish summer would never, never end!"

On the third floor, in her slope-ceilinged room, Mrs. Beavers tiptoed to and fro. She moved lightly and with purpose, closing the clasps of her suitcases stealthily. All had been attended to: she had had her week's pay today; the taxi was ordered for six-fifteen. She had no taste for scenes and would

be well out of the way by the time Marjorie came downstairs
to the empty kitchen with its lifeless stove and found the
letter which Mrs. Beavers was now composing in her head:

Dear Mrs. McLeod:

The working conditions in this household having become
intolerable . . .

A
Gift
of
Light

Mary Presbry enjoyed buying the presents for Rowena. She got her a yellow sweater and a silk scarf and a really good handbag—good enough for anyone—and of course some stockings. She thought about getting her a bathrobe, too, but decided against it.

She was pleased with her selections and wrapped them up in the same paper she used for all the other presents—gold, stamped with a silver-flake pattern. For several weeks before Christmas each year she constantly crackled about among papers and ribbons and string like a big nesting pigeon, and the packages grew into a crooked wall around her until she was sure that everybody had been remembered.

This time she nearly forgot Leonard. It was the day before Christmas when it was suddenly borne in upon her that Rowena had for some time been mentioning his name with a certain gentle emphasis. "Oh, God," she thought—really murmured to herself, moving her lips—"why do they always have to have children?"

Nevertheless, she put her galoshes on again and went out feeling petulant and put upon, but virtuous, too.

In the big toy store there was an atmosphere of peace after peril, as though large elements had penetrated and departed; gales of high velocity, perhaps. A few last-minute shoppers like herself picked over the depleted wares, and the saleswomen in attendance still had a dazed, muted look.

"The boy's about eleven," Mary told the one who drifted up to help her. "What do boys eleven like?"

"It depends on what's left," sighed the pale woman. "Practically everything's gone."

Mary looked with disfavor at knives and guns and decided in the end upon a flashlight with three different bulbs, red, green, and white.

"Boys always like flashlights," said the saleswoman, sighing.

Mary's good humor was restored; on the whole she enjoyed buying pleasures for people and could afford it.

That night when she gave Rowena her package, and an envelope with money in it, she told her not to come to work the next day. "I know you'll want to celebrate with Leonard. It's really the children's day, isn't it?"

"Thank you very, very much, Mrs. Presbry," Rowena said. She was never effusive.

"And here's a little gift for Leonard," Mary said, giving her the package (it was really rather large) which contained the flashlight.

"Oh, Mrs. Presbry, how lovely of you to remember him!" cried Rowena, her faint smile opening, widening, becoming a grin actually. When Mary thought of Rowena her mind's eye always saw her in profile, and in the profile the eye was always cast down, not in meekness or shame but in a sort of personal remoteness. Now, however, Rowena was looking straight at her, and the smile, the grin, was all for her, and she was warmed. Why are their teeth always so white? she wondered. But naturally it's the brown skin that makes them seem so much whiter than white people's.

Rowena had to wait quite a while for the bus. It was cold but she did not really mind. She loved the glittering packages in her arms and the many lighted Christmas trees along the avenue, and when the bus finally came and she had found a seat, she was pleased to see that even the bus was in the spirit of the evening, all lighted and crowded like a holiday ship, and everybody was carrying packages. The air was dense and cozy, and strangers wished each other Merry Christmas. When she got off at 117th Street Rowena felt very happy. She had great hopes for the New Year coming, and the passing one had not been unkind. She liked her place. For one who had wept from poverty and struggled for pennies and toiled in the roach-crackling fastnesses of stingy homes, it was wonderful to land at last in a day place that paid well, a little apartment all rosy and soft as silk, with just this one big lonesome dainty lady to look after.

Vicariously Rowena enjoyed the luxuries which were no more out of the way than bread and butter and soap to her employer. Tenderly she appreciated and cared for all of it, from the large, stuffed-silk back rest with the arms that Mrs. Presbry leaned back into while she ate her breakfast in bed to the wax flowers under glass bubbles and the tufted-satin sofa; from the dozens of hats that looked more like birds in nests or brides' bouquets than hats to the little colored ribbons that Mrs. Presbry laced through her pale-blue curls. Rowena regarded her as a sort of strange elderly toy: a big mama doll with beautiful dresses, living in a beautiful place; nice but not really real.

She was glad when she came to the building in which she lived; the packages were awkward to carry and her arms were tired. When she was halfway up the third flight of stairs, sighing and enduring, a door on the landing above flew open and Leonard was there to meet her.

"Hi, Mommy!"

"Hello, honey!"

"What's all those?"

"It's presents from Mrs. Presbry. One for you, too."

"Hot dog! Which one?"

"Now never mind. Tomorrow you'll know!"

Mary Presbry (when she considered him) imagined that Leonard would be rather a tall, mature Negro boy; Rowena had told her "He's smart!" But actually Leonard was small for his age, looking no more than eight or nine and weighing only sixty-five pounds. His skin was lighter than his mother's, his head was well-shaped, and his eyes between fantastically curled lashes had great brilliance and appeal, as though shining through a glaze of unshed tears.

His beauty was a perpetual surprise and blandishment to Rowena.

"You get a good lunch today, honey?"

"Tabby fixed it."

"Yes, I told her please."

"Look, Mommy, I did the tree."

"Honey, it's so pretty!"

They stood in the doorway looking at the small tree on the table, all hung with Santa Claus beard and red and blue bubbles.

The flashlight was the best thing. He took it into the closet and closed the door and tried the different lights and they all worked. He held it in his hand when he ate breakfast and kept it at his side when he lay on the floor reading the comics that Tabby had given him. Now and then when he felt impelled to take part in the action of the comic, he used the flashlight as a gun. "Keep your hands up, brother," he murmured. "Don't give me none of that, see, or I'll drill you."

"Oh, those comics!" said Rowena, stepping across him. "Oh, that trash!"

But Leonard did not hear her.

"You got it coming to you, mug," he said, and killed another victim before turning the page. That night after supper Rowena set up the ironing board and he took his flashlight down to the street to show it off.

"You be in by nine o'clock, hear," called Rowena from the landing, above his racketing descent.

But it was lonesome in the street; no kids were out. He stood on the stoop looking at the passing shadowy adults, at the windows with trees in them and the ones with wreaths. It was a fine night and the stars in the sky seemed to tremble and turn as though they were hung on threads and the air was moving them gently like Christmas tree ornaments.

Leonard went down the steps slowly, switching the beam of light first green, then red, rarely plain white, along the steps and palings. He sat down on the bottom step, which was cold, and waited for something to take place.

Two boys came along the street; old, big boys, maybe thirteen, maybe more. They were pushing each other and tripping each other and now and then they would stop and wrestle a little. The life that was in them both seemed to toss them about roughly like small boats on choppy seas. Their voices were betwixt and between a creak and a squawk. Leonard admired and feared them and stayed where he was without moving, hoping not to be seen. But in the next moment the bigger boy—very big he was—pushed the less big one right across the pavement and against Leonard.

"Watch it, kid, look out where you're going," the boy who had knocked into him said unreasonably. Leonard said nothing.

"What you doing hiding out here in the dark?" said the biggest boy, coming over.

"I ain't doing nothing," Leonard said.

"He ain't doing nothing, Satch," said the other one. "Come on; we gotta scram."

For reasons contradictory and unknown to himself, Leonard suddenly turned on the flashlight: first green, then red.

"Hey, look, Satch, he got a light!"

The biggest boy turned back. "Lemme see that light, kid."

He looked big, wolfish; he was smiling. He held out a big strong hand.

"No, I don't want to," Leonard said. He got up and began moving backward up the steps.

"You lemme looka that light you know what's good for you," Satch said, still grinning.

"No, listen, hey, I got an idea," the other one said, and he pulled Satch against him and whispered something.

"Ye-ah," said Satch, like a tough guy in the movies, drawing the word out long and knowing, on a declining note. "Listen, kid, how old are you?"

" 'Leven," said Leonard, still inclining up the steps.

"You sure runty for your age, ain't you?"

"He's no 'leven!" said the other one.

"I am so," said Leonard. "I was too 'leven, last October tenth."

"You sure runty."

"Okay, okay, you lea' me alone," said Leonard, who had now reached the top step and had his hand on the doorknob.

"No, listen, kid, we need a runty guy. We need a light, too. Listen, you got guts?"

"Sure I got guts," said Leonard, still with his hand on the knob but not turning it.

"You know how to keep your mouth shut?"

"Sure I know how to keep my mouth shut," said Leonard, who believed this to be true.

"You want to help us play a joke on some folks?"

"Naw, I don't know," Leonard said. "I got to go home."

"He say he had guts?" said the other one.

"This'll be a laugh, kid; it's for a gag," Satch said. "We'll give you something, something good, if you'll help us."

"What you going to give me?"

"You'll see, kid. It's—"

"It's money," said the other one. "It's dough."

"But maybe he ain't got the guts," said Satch.

"I got the guts," said Leonard, and he came down the steps.

Once when they were walking along the block he turned and looked back at the windows of the house where he lived and saw the Christmas lights in his mother's kitchen, and for a second he felt sad and scared and out of reach. But in a few minutes he was all right again, and after a while he felt fine. He was proud of being with these two big boys; he walked between them turning the flashlight off and on and boasting. Though the night was cold, he did not button up his mackinaw, he let it flap, and he left the earlaps of his cap turned up, as if any effort on his part toward order or protection would have been a confession of weakness. Besides, his companions were not as warmly dressed as he. Their wrists stuck out of raveled sleeves, their pants were torn and soiled, and their shoes scuffed. Leonard was a little annoyed by his own warm neat clothes.

"Where we going?" he said, when they came to the park. "How far off?"

"Not far off," Satch said. "Pretty close."

The park was all dark and restless and murmuring with night; it was an area of mystery, now, where not all the wild beasts were locked in cages. Leonard felt worried again.

"I got to get home pretty soon. I told—my father," he lied. Respect for a promise to one's mother would have sounded silly.

"What's the matter with you anyway?" said the other one. "He said it won't be long now. You heard him."

After a while they turned away from the windy avenue and walked several blocks east. On this street there were private houses, and tall apartment buildings, each with a long wealthy awning out in front, and glassed doorways which revealed a splendor of marble, carpeting, and fireplaces where nothing burned. Within these lighted lobbies, or bursting from them whistling like starlings, were the doormen whose coats and buttons were as uncompromising as those of the police. Satch and the other one and Leonard blew past them like the park's old leaves.

Christmas trees were everywhere: high up in windows, low down in doorways, and some of the private houses even had them outside on their front steps. Now and then there was a private house with no Christmas tree, no lights at all, and it was in front of one of these that Satch halted, looking to and fro along the street, before he ducked down the area steps.

"This is the one. Get down here quick. Get down quick and shut up now, keep still."

The areaway was a narrow rectangle onto which looked a barred window, and there was a cave-shaped doorway under the steps with an iron gate in front of it. Above the iron gate there was a space; a very little space.

"Think you can squeeze through that, kid?" Satch said.

"I don't want to," Leonard said. "I have to go home now. Honest. I *have* to."

"You get up there and shut up or you'll never go home no more," Satch said. He had cold big hands. With them he was holding on to Leonard's wrists, and in what he said there was the force of true meaning.

"What you want me to do?" Leonard said.

"We'll boost you up. You're runty enough to make it. Then open the gate from inside and let us in."

"Then can I go home?"

"And go squealin'? Naw, you stay with us. We need your light."

"What folks's house is this?" said Leonard.

"Keep your nose out of what folks's house it is. We know someone works here; we know about this house."

"It's for a gag like we told you," said the other one.

Leonard no longer believed him. He had never really believed him. He asked no more questions and began to clamber up the iron grille, their boosting hands behind him. It was a tight squeeze at the top—it ripped a button off his mackinaw —but in a moment he was through and had dropped into the little enclosure beyond. He turned the catch and opened the gate. The boys came in and closed it behind them. Satch took something out of his pocket.

"Shut up," he whispered. Close above them on the pavement footsteps passed, the ringing, even footsteps of an unsuspecting man. The footsteps sounded very lonely, yet very safe, walking away and away.

"Turn your flash on, kid. No, so it shows up the lock like this, see. Now hold it steady and keep your hand on the side of it, see, so the light don't shine out."

It was a little piece of celluloid Satch had. A little thin piece. He slid it into the crack of the door beside the lock and moved it. The catch of the lock moved; the lock was willing to surrender, but the door would not give up.

"Goddam thing's got a bolt," Satch said. But nothing was going to stop him now. He seized the flashlight from Leonard and with its butt end smashed the pane of glass nearest the lock. The many icy sounds of shattering and falling glass were sharp as pain. They stood there, waiting for the noise to have its consequence. But nothing happened. Finally Satch put his hand through the ragged aperture, found the bolt, and the door swung open and they were in the house.

He turned the light off and they stood there, listening to the great stillness of the house and smelling its unfamiliar smell. After a while they began to creep forward. Satch still had the light and from time to time he turned it on—long enough to see the hall and the stairs before them. But mostly they moved in the dark.

"I don't think it's nobody home," he said. "But we got to take it easy."

Behind them, through the broken door, a cold little brooklet of air streamed into the deep warm house.

"Stick close to us, you," the other one hissed at Leonard, but Leonard was right at his heels. Their steps made no sound, for the carpet was deep and thick. When Satch struck his foot against a piece of furniture, when the first stair creaked, they froze together, the three of them, and their heartbeats were like the feet of fugitives pounding through forests. Leonard felt sick at his stomach and the tears kept gathering against his eyes.

On the next floor they grew bolder: Satch turned on the flashlight and a room came into life. There was a piano, and there were big chairs and many tables with little things on them. All the mute objects in the dusky room seemed to Leonard to be staring and disapproving like old people who have been startled out of sleep by the noise of children. When it was dark again he had a feeling that all the furniture would become active, that it would come after them silently, rocking and lumbering. He did not want to be last and pushed ahead between Satch and the other one, but the other one snatched him back by the collar. "Stay where you belong!"

Satch seemed to know where he was going. In the blackness they crawled up another mossy, softly creaking stairway. The

closed air had a smell of sweetness and idleness, and in the
big boys a certain excitement now began to have its effect.
There was whispering between them and a lessening of cau-
tion.

Leonard followed them from the landing into a room at
the front of the house. There the blinds were slitted with
faint light from the street; Satch went and closed them and
the other one softly shut the door and said, "Now!" Leonard
could hear the little sound his hand made as it explored the
wall, and then the room sprang into light.

A great pink place it was. There were silk coverlets on the
beds, the rug had flowers woven into it, the windows were
dressed up like rich ladies in party dresses, and there were
looking glasses everywhere. Leonard's interest edged his fear a
little to one side. He put out his forefinger to stroke the satin
coverlet and drew a deep snuffling breath to fill his lungs with
the room's itching-sweet smell of perfume. Dazed with warmth
and softness he stood still, snuffling and gaping, but the other
two were not wasting time in staring; they were quiet and
businesslike and busy. And now Leonard saw (he had always
guessed) what was going on, and he was afraid again. Satch
and the other one were pulling out the bureau drawers and
opening the little boxes and stuffing things into their pockets.
The other one found a big handbag with money in it, and
hanging out of Satch's back pants pocket there was the loop
of a necklace. They opened the cupboard doors and tore down
the many dresses on their hangers and pulled the shoes out
of the shoe bags and the hats out of the hat boxes, and Satch
tried on one of the hats and they snorted with laughing.
They seemed to be crackling like fire with excitement and
triumph and rage, and then they went into the adjoining
room and Leonard could hear them in there, stirring and
whispering and thumping and trying not to laugh. He was left
alone in all the rosy dishevelment, but he could not run away;
his feet were rooted to the flowered carpet and he did not care
whether he was crying or not.

When they came back they went over the room once more,

ransacking every corner to make certain that nothing had been overlooked.

After a while the other one said, "Come on. Let's get out." Then he said it again. "Come on, come on, we got it now. Come on, scram." But something had got into Satch; he was wild, pulling the covers off the beds, tossing the pillows on the floor, jerking the bureau drawers out of their cases and dumping them upside down.

"I'll fix 'em," he was muttering. "This'll fix 'em! They think they got it; they think they goina keep it; I'll show 'em!"

He tipped over the perfume bottles on the dressing table, and seizing a lipstick that was there he wrote a word big on the wall. Leonard knew that word. It was a bad word.

"Cut it out, Satch; you screwy?" said the other one. "We got it now, ain't we? Come on now, Satch. Listen, come on."

All at once, above the sounds of whispered argument and muffled tears, there were other sounds not of their making, a door opening, footsteps overhead somewhere. . . .

For one icy moment they saw one another's faces, and then they were out of the room, noisy, reckless, falling down the stairs; Leonard last, as usual.

Above them a voice yelled, the deep hall glared with light, and the stairs at the top of the house began to thunder and quake. The boys' flight downward was an endless dreamlike progress, for while their heads and bodies were thin and effortless as air, their feet had turned to logs and stones.

Leonard, being last, was the only one to see the man. He dared to turn once, and there, staring downward from the landing above him, was the big man he would never forget; the big man in blue pajamas with his gray hair sleep-disheveled, and his mouth open. He was shouting, and his fist was raised to strike or to kill. . . .

Satch got to the door first and yanked it open and flung open the gate beyond. The cold night gave them speed, though behind them the man still came, barefoot and yelling. One or two who were passing stopped and stared, all initiative wiped from their faces, and an apartment-house doorman came out under his awning, blowing a whistle for the cops. But Satch and Leonard and the other one were too young and light and scared to be caught. They skipped across the avenue between the hooting cars and lost themselves in the park. There they crouched their way through thickets and under bridges. It was wild and windy; among tossing branches the street lights danced and disappeared. There were dark shadows and people moving like shadows, and all around the rectangle of wilderness and dingy woods the city lay in a great frame of light.

Leonard stumbled after the big boys. His recent tears turned cold and dried against his cheeks and his breathing came easier. He wiped his nose on the cuff of his mackinaw and asked a question: "Where we going now?"

They had half-forgotten him. Satch turned on him. "Beat it now, small fry. Get out."

"Gimme my light, then."

"Forget your light. Scram, I said."

"You gimme my light."

It was surprising that the other one came to his defense. "Aw, go on; give the kid his light. Hadn't been for him we never could of done it."

"I ain't got the light," Satch said.

"You ain't *got* it!"

"I lef' it in the house. Must have. I ain't got it now."

"You big dumb jerk," Leonard said, his voice quavering with misery and outrage.

Great weariness caught up with him. Whether the flashlight was still in the house they had left, or in the big raw hand of some cop, or, as he suspected, safely hidden in one of Satch's pockets, he, at least, had lost it. All·he had instead was the gray-haired man chasing him downstairs forever. He turned his back on the two big boys and started to go away.

"Hold it, small fry," Satch said. He came after him and took hold of his arm. "We're going to give you your cut. You did okay." He put a bill in Leonard's chilly, unenthusiastic hand. "If they ask questions when you spend it tell 'em your auntie gave it to you for Christmas. Watch it going home. Don't stay on no paths; keep to the bushes and watch it when you come out of the park."

"Okay," Leonard said sadly, putting the bill in his pocket.

Satch's loose hold on his arm tightened suddenly. His face, with its dark wild eyes and the grin which was merry only to himself, came close to Leonard's. "And if you let on what we done, if you even say you ever saw us, see, we'll come after you. We know where you live, and if you squeal—"

"I ain't gonna squeal," Leonard said.

"—and if you squeal we'll come up the stairs and we'll tie you up and pull out your eyelashes and pull out the hairs in your eyebrows and we'll pin your ears to your head with safety pins—"

"You le' go me!" cried Leonard, and with a last prayer flung at whoever it was in heaven—there was surely someone—whose only concern was Leonard, he tore himself free and began to run.

He could hear Satch laughing, and the other one said, "Aw, leave him go," and nobody chased him but he kept on running anyway.

It took him a long time to get out of the park. Once, behind him, he heard a police whistle, feet running, and voices, and he hid for a while between a rock and a tree. He did not know if the cops had caught up with Satch and the other one. He felt cold and tired and wished to be home.

When he emerged at 110th Street he met with no trouble, though he had expected it, and, filled with apprehension, he began the long walk home. When he got home—if he ever did—he would tell his mother what had happened. She would know what to do—whether to send him to jail or forgive him. He sighed deeply and put his cold hands into his pockets where one of them closed in a guilty reflex on the bill. Trouble, trouble, trouble, all for just one buck. The flashlight was worth more.

At first every footstep he heard was the step of pursuit and every glance that fell upon him was the glance of an accuser.

He was all aprickle and in a sweat of guilt and fright, but as the long blocks were traveled and home drew nearer, he began to relax. Two blocks from his own street he was able to pause under the quavering marquee lights of the Colonial Palace movie theater and look furtively at the bill.

He could feel his heart open and shut. In his hand, where he had expected to see a dollar, he found a ten-dollar bill. Satch had given him ten dollars.

Never before had he held this much money in his own hand; with the event a whole new range of achievement was revealed to him. He could have another flashlight; he could have one hundred comics. He could buy a dog or take a ride in an airplane or get a present for his mother and a suit with long pants for himself. The choices were infinite, but beneath their dazzle he was able to make a plan: He would tell his mother that some big boys, strangers, had taken the light—it was true, it was true—but he would not tell her anything else; he would not speak of the ten dollars. Or perhaps, later, he would say that he had found it.

He turned in at his street, carried on new current. It was suddenly necessary to skip, to jump over the cracks and hop on one foot. Smart people don't have to stay poor.

Many blocks to the south Mary Presbry turned over in bed and looked at her clock; it was still too early to tell whether or not this was going to be a good night. She felt hopeful, lonesome, and trustful, and yawned loudly, like a child, in the darkness. A faint warmth of satisfaction came to her as she thought of the day just past and of the Christmas pleasure she had given to all those whose lives touched hers.

In Rowena's kitchen the metallic bird walk of the clock was beginning to be alarming; it was marching too fast toward a late hour. She put down her iron and listened, and then she went and opened the window, leaning far out and looking down into the street. There she saw Leonard hopping along the pavement with his mackinaw flapping and his hands in his pockets. Knowing him, she was surprised that he was not showing off the flashlight. Probably he had broken it already. Her anxiety gave way to relieved exasperation as she drew her head in and banged the window down. Kids! she thought. You give them a present they're crazy about and first thing they do they always break it.

The
Olive
Grove

All they want is just the one thing," said Enid Hasher, shaking pebbles out of her shoe. "They're all the same, just the one thing on their minds."

Coral's glance was guarded but incredulous. Mrs. Hasher was fifty-two and had a face that looked as though it had been carved with a chisel by a Pilgrim; "decisive" was a word that would describe her features; "sharp" was another. She was wearing royal-blue pedal pushers, a red shirt, and a cap with a beak. Between the edges of her pedal pushers and the tops of her socks her bare calves had an innocent, uncarnal look; her eyes had that look, too, when she removed her pince-nez to press the bridge of her nose, where two painful little dents were printed. Beyond her the hot, hard canyon wall rose steeply, spiked with cardon cacti, and starting with lizards.

"Ever since Mr. Hasher died, I've run into that sort of thing. You'd like a friendly date now and then, just *friendly* —dinner and a movie or something—but, oh, no, that's not *their* idea!"

"It must be awful," murmured Coral, young and safely married, looking down in embarrassment at her brown shins. All of them—the men working on the car below, even old Mrs. Clove strolling up the road—were sunburned from their days on the Gulf. But Mrs. Hasher, white as milk, did not care for boats or sun, and only flew down to the fishing lodge for visits with her sister, who was the proprietor's wife.

None of the members of this expedition knew each other well, and perhaps it was this sense of friendship forced upon them, as on shipboard, that was causing Mrs. Hasher to discuss her problem with a virtual stranger. Not that Coral believed in the problem. Heavens, at fifty-two? Never. It must be self-delusion.

From the angle of the canyon below them came a scraping, a metallic knocking, and the sound of men's voices. Twenty minutes ago, jolting over the mountain road, paved as informally as a river-bed, they had finally struck a boulder that was too much for them; the car stuck fast. The three men, Pepe, the driver, Mr. Beau Branson, with his Leica swinging, and Mr. Massaccio, the dark Italian, had prowled about the car, peering beneath it, kicking at the boulder, preparing for struggle while the women watched comfortably. And then suddenly, from what seemed a wilderness, two men appeared, appropriate as saints. They were wearing sombreros, and one of them had a shovel. Pepe greeted them like brothers.

The heat in the canyon had a still ferocity. Mrs. Clove, walking slowly up the road, could feel tears of perspiration pushing past her hatband, but she enjoyed the heat, and always had, even as a girl. She picked her way carefully among the stones, thinking of snakes. Beside the road, and now and then across it, trickled a string of water in which an edging of green weed lay wagging. Bending over, she could see nothing of her reflection but the outline of her Mexican hat. She was glad she had decided on this trip today. Having flown down from California with her son and daughter-in-law, ten days ago, she felt that she needed a respite as much from them, whom she loved, as from the blazing days on the water which she had come to dread.

Each of them today had come alone. Coral without her husband, Mr. Branson without the two prankish boys of sixty who were his fishing companions, Mr. Massaccio without his leathery American wife. All who had remained behind preferred fish to churches, and were frank to say so.

"But not you, Mr. Branson?" Mrs. Clove had been a little surprised.

He showed his square enduring teeth in a grin. "Honey, I've had it. Marlin, two hundred pounds; grouper, two seventy-five. Sails all makes and sizes. And bonito! *Sierra! Cabrilla!* Everything there is but turtles. Anyway, I wanna get some shots of this mission."

No one knew why Mr. Massaccio had come along. No one knew much about him in any case except that he was an Italian reaching middle age, married to a woman who had already achieved it and who looked rich. He spoke very little English but made up for it by smiling in many different ways. His dark eyes, long and fish-shaped, were also used as a form of language.

Mrs. Clove took off her hat and dried her forehead. A butterfly sailed over the tiny stream, lit on a stone, and fanned its foreign-looking wings.

"Okay, people! Let's *go-o-o!*" Beau Branson's shout struck echoes from the rocks.

Mrs. Clove turned hastily and started back, spurred by a childish fear of being left behind.

"What I'd really like," Mrs. Hasher was telling Coral as Mrs. Clove overtook them, "is to get married again. Some nice retired fellow. I'm just so tired of living alone."

The three women slipped and hobbled down the stony road to resume their places in the car. Coral sat in back between Enid Hasher and Mrs. Clove; as the youngest and slimmest she had to pay for those blessings by taking the worst seat.

The car jolted on again, always ascending. The road grew worse all the time, elbowing around outcroppings, becoming nothing but a narrow shelf between mountainside and steep descending cliff. Below, to the left, great arid valleys opened out.

"Pepe, you don't think we'll meet another car, do you?" pleaded Mrs. Hasher.

Busy mastering the road, he did not trouble to reply.

Mrs. Clove, in the outside seat, refrained from looking at the view, studying, instead, the backs of the men's heads: Beau Branson's frankly bald and burned; Mr. Massaccio's showing an ambushed crescent of scalp between dark strands; Pepe's nothing but a neck and a sombrero.

Now and then Mr. Massaccio would turn and look back at the women with one of his conversational smiles—smiling most often, most directly, at Coral, Mrs. Clove noticed. Coral noticed this, too, and looked away. Though she was thirty, she looked much younger, and though she was soundly married and had two stout children at home to prove it, she retained a pensive, virginal air that well became her.

The road continued its relentless climb. When the radiator began to boil Pepe stopped the car and they got out. They were on a high, bright plateau. Far away, at the bottom of a cleft in the mountains, lay a wedge of sea.

Mrs. Hasher plucked her damp shirt away from her ribs. "I'm sweating from nerves as much as from the heat," she confided to Mr. Branson. "I just hope this church is worth it!"

"Mission. —Well, it's mighty old. Poor now, though. They have no priest; the padre comes up Sundays from Santa Eulalia to conduct the mass."

"Over that *road?* Well, I suppose if you're a priest you don't feel it the same."

In the canyons below, the *ocatillas* were tagged with scarlet. Century plants rose out of their viper leaves like big decorated masts. Mr. Massaccio held his tossing hair against his scalp and smiled and smiled. Edging toward Coral, he nodded at the view. "Is beautful?"

"Beautiful," she said, though that was not the adjective she would have chosen. Strange, bitter, thrilling, would be better ones, she thought. The air had an aromatic smell that tickled her nostrils; the hot wind stroked her nape. She had never been out of the United States before, and was dazzled and wary, like a cat set down in an unfamiliar meadow.

The rest of the drive was uneventful; the road zigged and zagged but climbed no longer. Presently they met a flock of

goats and a goatherd, all smoking with dust, and then a man
stuck onto a tiny donkey like a clothespin.

"And there's the mission, finally!" said Beau Branson, un-
limbering his Leica.

It stood at the end of an empty plaza, a high square building
with one domed tower. It was the color of the mountains behind it, having been made of their rock, and had more the
look of a fortress or a prison than a church, Mrs. Clove
thought. It seemed to her that compared to it, the New England churches of her background had an almost feminine and
social grace, the expression of something not quite serious.
This building was serious. It was harsh and commanding.

As soon as they stepped across the threshold it was cool.
The air, as contained as air in a cellar or a tomb, was still
stained with an old smell of incense. There were no pews or
benches. The stone floor echoed under their feet, and there
was a dizzy thrumming from the wasps whose clay nests
studded the walls and hung like spools from the tops of the
open windows.

The nave was narrow, high-shouldered, and austere. But
austerity ended at the chancel, where a vast crested altar rose
to the ceiling, paneled with paintings and fuming with gold.
After all they had seen that was dry, bleached, dusty, the
shock of its flamboyance had the effect of noise, Mrs. Clove
thought, loud but harmonious, like a trumpet fanfare. The
Leica clicked; Mr. Massaccio genuflected. "Stunning," said
Mrs. Hasher.

A swallow flew in one window and out another.

Beyond the altar rail stood a figure of the Virgin, dressed
in cracking brocade and wearing a crown. On her left hand
rested the Holy Infant, small as a bee.

"Is beautiful?" said Mr. Massaccio, edging toward Coral.

"Beautiful," Coral repeated, edging toward Mrs. Clove.

When they climbed the tower stair, "to take in the view"
at Mrs. Hasher's suggestion, they saw that the white plaster
walls were scratched with names and dates.

"But all Spanish names. Where are the Americans?" said Coral.

"We are the advance guard," replied Mrs. Clove, holding the handrail and watching her step.

At the landing there was an open door; beyond it the flat stone roof. They felt the sudden weight of noonday on their heads when they stepped out, and the parapet was too hot to lean against. Down in the plaza, Pepe was leaning against the car, talking and spitting with a baked old stick of a man.

"Town sure looks dead," Beau Branson observed, aiming his camera at it anyway.

The crowding mountains bristled with cactus. Broken beer bottles flashed in the churchyard, and everywhere, though out of sight, wild pigeons were booming with a hoarse explosive sound that bore no resemblance to the utterances of any pigeons they had ever heard before.

Jab! Stab! Burn and break! That's what this country says, thought Mrs. Clove, whose own country said nothing to her but Remember. Endure. Control. Remember.

She smiled under her broad hat, thinking of a moment earlier in the day. They had left Santa Eulalia far behind and could see nothing on either side but the sparse, spiked forests of the desert. The scene had reminded Beau Branson of a lecture he had once heard at the Rotary Club:

"Seems there was this young couple the fellow was telling about that made a bet they could survive for—I forget how long, but it was *weeks* or *months*—with nothing in the way of tools or provisions. Just a machete. How about that? Just a machete. And, by golly, they won the bet! When they got thirsty they'd open up a cactus, see (there's a kind you can), and drink the juice off. And they learned how to make snares out of fibers and stuff and trapped their food."

"I guess you could make out," Enid Hasher had mused. "Of course, you'd miss your green vegetables."

The smile faded from the old woman's face. What am I doing here? she thought suddenly. This questioning happened to her often lately. She would be sailing forward, carried by enthusiasm, and all at once the wind would die and she would find herself becalmed, at a loss. The only thing to do then was to grasp at some idea of comfort, or seize on a reason that was not frightening. I believe I must be hungry, she thought now. Yes, that's probably the trouble.

"Isn't it nearly time for lunch?"

"Oh, I hope so. I'm *famished!*" Coral cried, sounding too girlish to her own ears. She took off her sombrero to fan her face and her fair hair lighted up. Mr. Massaccio's smile sagged a little as he stared.

"Where in the world can we eat it, though?" Mrs. Hasher demanded. "You just can't eat in a church!"

But when they came down they found that Pepe had had his instructions. He led them across the plaza to a house set in the wall of houses, and knocked at a cactus-wood gate which was opened at once by a man with a harsh gray beard. He smiled and bowed. *"Bienvenido."* Beyond in the open passage sat his old father, hands knotted around a stick, eyes milky with cataract.

"Poor soul," Enid Hasher said, dutifully.

Beyond the passage there was a roofed veranda where chickens were pecking at crumbs on a littered table, and from this they stepped down into the deep unexpected shade of an olive grove.

The trees were spaced well apart, thick girthed, with mighty buttresses and flailing tails; ancient, grotesque, and splendid. Their leaves were so dense that it was twilight under them; one could hardly believe in the chips of brilliance that showed between the leaves, and the hoarse doves seemed to call from a great distance.

Beau Branson slapped a twisted trunk. *"Viejo, si?"*

"Muy viejo, si, señor. Dos cientos." The bearded man held up two fingers.

"Two centuries old, the guy says!"

At the heart of the grove was its reason for being: gently flowing water in a stone flume. Its brown surface was bloomed with indigo and speckled with leaves. Small wooden chairs had been set out beside it, and Pepe sank beer bottles in the water to cool. Waiting, the travelers wandered in the shade. The grove was so ancient and so still that they spoke quietly there, as they had done in the mission. As well as by the olive trees, it was shaded by massive fig trees with leaves like cobblers' aprons.

"Now you can see why they used fig leaves in the Bible," said Mrs. Hasher sagely. "This must be the kind they had in mind. Your California fig leaf would not have been sufficient."

A group of children gathered in the shadows to watch them eat. Their town was so remote, so out of touch, that they had not learned about begging. They watched gravely, without giggling or talking. Now and then one of them, a tiny boy in a sombrero, would hawk his throat clear and spit like a man of fifty.

The others did not talk, either, at first. They were glad to sit still, eating their lunch, recovering from the morning's long assault of light. The water flowed silently in its stone sleeve, and there was no breath of air to stir the leaves. A rooster approached elegantly on yellow trident feet, shaking his comb, darting his topaze eye. Behind him came the frumpy hen.

"You'd just know those were Mexican chickens," Mrs. Hasher said, tossing crumbs. "I don't know why, but they look entirely different from chickens in the States."

Mrs. Clove ate with relish; already she felt better.

But Coral was not hungry, after all, and gave her sandwiches to the children. She was preoccupied, troubled by the Italian and by herself. All morning—in the car, in the mission, in the grove, in all shadowed places—his eyes had turned to her. Even when she refused to look at them the eyes persisted in her mind; almond-shaped, glittering, like two bits of faïence, as lustrous and as hard.

After lunch Mrs. Clove and Mrs. Hasher strolled away. I ought to go with them, thought Coral, and yet she did not. When Mr. Massaccio approached and touched her wrist she was not surprised, and yet she started.

"We walk?" he said, smiling; and she stood up and moved away beside him, helpless and obedient, feeling languid, strange to herself, like one of the dry little olive leaves that slipped along the surface of the flume.

Among the children there was a tiny girl in a long faded dress. Her black hair hung in tangled threads on her brow and neck, and her eyes were large and serious.

Beau Branson took a peso from his pocket. "Look here, honey," he said, kneeling down before her and proffering the friendliest aspect of his teeth and glasses. She did not draw away but put her finger in her mouth for courage, and her eyes grew larger. He held the peso up. "See? Money. Mon-ey. Say it, honey. Say it, *chiquita*. Money, see? Mon-ey."

She took her finger out of her mouth.

"Mon-ee," she whispered.

"That's right! *Bueno!* Here. And here's another. Say it again."

She put her hand out.

"No, no!" He held it away. "You must ask for it, see? Money!"

"Mon-ee! Mon-ee!" Her voice had real feeling in it now.

"*Si! Si! Muy bien!*" He laughed delightedly, and gave her the coin. She laughed, too, showing her baby teeth and stamping her dirty little feet.

And now the others took it up, jumping and piping, "Mon-ee? Mon-ee? Mon-ee?" He emptied his pockets of Mexican and American coins. "Now, come with me. *Vamos, niños.* I wanna get a picture of you kiddies in the sun."

There had not been enough to give to all of them; the spitter in the sombrero flung himself against a tree in silent grief.

Coral and Mr. Massaccio emerged from the shadow to cross a patch of hot grass snapping with insects, and found another shadow under another tree. In there, where water had spilled over from the flume, forget-me-nots were blooming, deep blue because there was no sun to bleach them. The olive root that hid among them like a snake caused Coral to stumble, only hastening the thing that was to happen. The Italian caught her, held her, swung her around to face him, and murmuring something in his own language, took her in his arms.

At first she tried to resist, then pretended to try, then folded her arms around his neck. He embraced her fiercely, almost as if punishing her, and she—it was strange, but she was infected by his fierceness and found herself behaving as she had never in her life behaved with her husband. She felt a wish to bite, pinch, grapple, as if there were anger in this kind of loving. And indeed, "loving" was not the word for it, she knew.

Walking quietly, puffing on a cigarette (she had never learned to inhale), Mrs. Clove caught sight of them, stared for an instant, and retreated in haste. When she was safely out of sight she stopped and leaned against a tree.

The olive trees with their flailing trunks now seemed to her, as they had often seemed to others, to be imprisoned in attitudes of lust and longing. And what else were the pigeons booming about in the sunshine?

> Fish, flesh, or fowl, commend all summer long
> Whatever is begotten, born, or dies . . .

Hardly noticing what she was doing she put out the cigarette and went to the flume to cool her hands in the water.

> Consume my heart away; sick with desire
> And fastened to a dying animal
> It knows not what it is . . .

He said it all, she thought, and no one ever said it better; but beneath a superficial touch of pride at having been able to put her hand on the right quotation at the right time, there was the bald, tedious fact of what she had to face, the truth in the words.

The water was nearly as warm as the air, but it felt like

silk and sounded pleasant when she played her hand in it. One must be a parent to oneself in old age, she thought. No one else will be. There, there, little one, cool your hands, or light a cigarette, or take a drink, or open the new book, or plant the new plant. These tabs of pleasure must do for you. Enough of them will make a coverlet—full of holes, perhaps, but better than nothing on a chilly night.

"Oh, it's *not* as bad as that," she murmured to herself. The parent must speak to reassure the child. "No, of course, it's not," she said, lifting her hand out of the water and watching the wet sparkle of her diamond ring.

"Talking to yourself, honey?" Beau Branson came striding toward her, grinning. The Leica swung against his chest like a mayor's locket.

"Yoo-hoo!" called Enid Hasher. "Where *is* everybody?"

The two in the shadow sprang apart.

"Oh, there you are. You might have answered. I was getting scared you'd all gone off without me, I'm *telling* you!"

Mr. Massaccio had lost his smile, and Coral's face looked strange, but Mrs. Hasher noticed nothing. She had news of her own and as they walked back through the grove she imparted it to Coral. "You know that fellow with the beard? The one that let us in? Well, honestly! When I passed him back there a while ago, just *as* I passed him, he"—she lowered her voice and leaned toward Coral—"he reached out and *pinched* me! Oh, listen, even these Mexican men! They seem so quiet and polite and all, but they're just the same as all the rest!"

Though she spoke indignantly she did not look indignant, only rather pink; rather pleased, Coral thought.

The plaza was still burning hot. They waited there while Pepe stowed away the picnic things. The light had deepened; the mountains were no longer gray but gold, and the mission was gold. The distant shred of sea was gentian blue.

Mr. Massaccio had regained his smile. His wrist watch glittered as he smoothed his hair, and his long eyes looked secretly at Coral. There is time, his sure smile seemed to say. We will find a way.

But, no, we will not, thought Coral. That was in *there*. That was *then*. Nevertheless, she drew closer to Mrs. Clove, who patted her arm. The poor child's given herself a fright, thought the old woman. Oh, what a waste, what a silly waste, to make ourselves this worthless gift so often in our lives! If we have nothing to be afraid of we construct something. One short day on earth, and that's how we insult it. Wasteful. Sinful.

"I'm glad to leave that place," she said to Coral.

"So am I!"

"Why? It was so picturesque." Mrs. Hasher was reproachful.

"Yes, but too old. Even for me. The place has been alive too long. One old tree, or two or three; that's always a pleasant sight, but when you find yourself surrounded by a crowd of them, a *host* of them, all breathing down on you, it's oppressive. They're such a living example of the last word. No, I don't care for it. I feel the same about the redwoods."

Beau Branson was the last to join them. The children tagged at his heels, and when they saw the other people in the car they began to hop and shout. "Mon-ee? Mon-ee?" The big bald man smiled at them gently, almost shyly, charmed with his handiwork. *"Adios, niños.* Good-by."

The homeward road twisted in such a way that now and then it offered them another view of the mission, but each time the authority of the building was diminished, and the last glimpse showed them something no bigger than a thimble.

Mrs. Clove was soon tormented by drowsiness, but refused to permit it the upper hand and firmly disciplined her yawns. No one should be seen asleep but children, she thought to herself. And lovers, by each other . . . Oh, stop that line of thought, for heaven's sake! Drop it! I'm tired to death of the whole subject. Bored to death. Let's see. What is there? Yes. When we get back I think I'll have a swim in the pool. And after that a cocktail; two cocktails (but not three), and then dinner; that grouper last night was perfectly delicious.

Hour
of
Loss

Alida was gravely ill; so was Germian. Alida was so ill that her eyes would no longer close; hitting her on the head or shaking her had no effect: her strong-blue eyes with stationary pupils stared fixedly at the ceiling. She lay on a cloud of rose-pink fluff which had been plucked by hand, after dark, from a blanket at the Hotel Blackstone in Chicago. Germian had no such mattress; she lay naked on the bare slats of her bed, but over her she had a coverlet of golden lamé, and if her eyes would not close it was only because she had no eyes. She had no scalp, either; her head was empty as an eggshell and as pink inside as outside.

"Let's have the funeral now," said Dody.

"We can't. Alida isn't dead yet," Hester said.

"Germian is. Her heart stopped beating just this minute."

"Well, Alida isn't quite. We'll have to have the funeral after lunch, and anyway we won't be hurried then."

Dody stopped arguing; Hester was the guest, after all, and besides she had the strongest will. If one were going to be best friends with Hester one would have to accept that from the first.

"She's very low, though, very low," said Hester, in a voice that made Dody's spine creep. It was just this kind of remark that made Hester's friendship so worth while. Into a dull day and a dull game she could inject flashes of purple and crimson; she knew how to talk and even act like a grownup, without the curse of being one.

"If we use Mike's dump truck and bus we'll have to let him in the funeral," Dody said.

"That's all right, he and Selden can be the pallbearers. Even Loie can be in it if she wants."

"She won't know what it is. She's too young yet to know you die."

"That doesn't matter. Now, come on; let's ask your mother if she has any black cloth to put on the cars."

"Why do you two little girls want to play about dying on a lovely spring day like this?" said Dody's mother, but her Aunt Perley, who was taking the curlers out of her red hair, said, "They're just finding an outlet for their aggressions, honey. It's a healthy sign."

"Honestly, Perley, the things they taught you at the University!" But it was clear that Dody's mother had respect for her young sister-in-law, or for the things she had learned; she began rooting through her piece bag for some black material. "The amount of psychology you've soaked up! If I knew even half of what you do I'd never dare to raise a family, I swear."

"Probably better that you don't," said Aunt Perley, combing out her fiery curls. "You're instinctive; you act instinctively. And luckily you're healthy; you do a minimum amount of harm."

"My soul and body," said Dody's mother. "No matter what you do these days you get no credit. Here, girls, here's some black silk-velvet I had in a housecoat years ago, and this black satin—where did this black satin come from? I think it was the lining of a coat of Edna's."

"The funeral will be at half-past two," said Hester, "and everybody's invited."

"Count on us," said Aunt Perley, in her teasing grown-up way. "You can count on us, girls, in your hour of loss."

Hester and Dody trimmed the truck and bus with doleful. swags and then went out to find flowers for further decoration. T'e screen door twanged behind them with an exhilarating sound of summer—the door had only been on a week—

and they went down to the orchard, leaping, hilarious on their mournful errand.

Hester had never seen the valley in spring before. She was here now because she had been sick for a long time in the winter: "With penicillin and a trained nurse and the doctor every single day. I was very low. Now they want me to get my strength back." Hester tossed her hair as she said this; she was always tossing it irritably back over her shoulder as though she felt affronted, imposed upon, by having to wear it on her head at all. Actually she was very proud of her hair; it was heavy and straight and hung almost to her waist. . . . Every year she came to visit Dody on her way to see her father, but usually it was later on, in June. "Father has me in the summer and vacations, and Mother has me for the school year," she had explained to Dody. "I'm the only one they've got, so I guess they have to divide me up exactly even."

Dody had not a word to say. Her case was different; she understood that her parents had all they wanted of their children, all they needed, just by living in the house with them. That was all right, it was just like eating or breathing, an everyday thing, but there was nothing interesting about it.

The apple orchard was in full blossom and purring with bees; the lilacs were beginning, too, and all the grass was new and soft and unresistant like pieces of ribbon. Every meadow was a different green except for the ones that were chocolate brown, and they had tips of green coming out of them in rows. Big dark-blue shadows of clouds swam over them, and the wind was full of spent petals and cabbage butterflies.

There were violets under the trees; Hester and Dody picked a lot of them. In the center of each violet were some small black streaks that made it look as though someone had marked it with pen and ink. They picked lilacs, too, though the clusters were almost all buds, hard as beads.

"Hester? Dody? Come and get it!" called Aunt Perley's voice, and they came slowly up the path, dizzy with sunshine and the smell of flowers.

Lunch was really dinner in Dody's house. Everyone ate together except Loie, who was upstairs sleeping in her crib. Even Dody's father came, because he stayed home and worked on the farm all day instead of in an office. And then there were Selden and Mike and their mother, and Aunt Perley and Uncle Gill, who were visiting, and of course Dody and Hester. Winona brought everything in from the kitchen and just put it on the table; big hillocks and hummocks of food. Hester ate some of everything, even things nobody could get her to eat at home, like Brussels sprouts and turnip and pie. She ate them all, though not with the steady purpose of Selden and Mike, who got right into their food and wore it on their faces.

"If you think this is bad, you should see them at corn-on-the-cob time," Dody said. "Selden always has a kernel in his ear and one on the side of his cheek."

For dessert, this day, there was applesauce with coconut cake. Hester folded a piece of hers in her paper napkin.

"I've got a pickle, too, and a little piece of meat," she whispered to Dody. "I'm going to put them all in the box with Alida so she won't be hungry."

"How can she be hungry if she's dead?"

"How do you know what it's like to be dead? You might get hungry. I'm not going to take any chances."

"Well, all right. Germian can have some jelly beans," said Dody, eating up her cake.

The funeral was late, of course. The mourners had forgotten to dig the graves, and then there was the question of finding the right coffins. In the end Alida had a Mrs. Snyder candy box, and Germian had the box that Mike's blue Keds had come in.

The grownups straggled out onto the terrace, half reluctant, half amused. Their moods did not matter; the grownups were nothing but the background, the audience. Dody's father was the only one who was not present; he was far afield on the bucking tractor, shouting above its racket to the hired men.

Petals spun and flickered from the trees; the funeral procession emerged from the house. First came Mike, crouching and pushing the dump truck which was swathed in black and

stuck with sprigs of flowers. On it Alida lay in her nest of
pink wool with her blue eyes staring at the sky. Next came
Selden, also crouching, with the bus, on top of which Germian
was lashed. Her golden coverlet was blinding in the sunshine.
("Oh, Hester, must I bury her with her cover on?" Dody had
entreated. "Well, you have to make some sacrifice, Dody. You
don't want her to think you're anxious to get rid of her, do
you?" "No. Only—gee.") After that came Loie, wobbling and
tottering and pulling the block wagon full of dolls and bears
and gone-to-seed rabbits and pandas. She kept dropping the
handle of the wagon and waddling off in irrelevant directions.
"Loie get back in line," cried the outraged voices, but she was
as impervious to the will of others as a kitten or a bird; each
time they'd have to go and bring her back by hand.

Then came the two chief mourners, Dody and Hester, each
carrying a coffin which rattled. In Germian's were the jelly
beans; in Alida's, cake, meat, a pickle, a large ball of tinfoil,
a small piece of Hester's hair.

The graves were ready, side by side under one of the middle
apple trees. The procession halted and the grownups halted,
too, in a yawning, haphazard way.

"First we all have to say the Lord's Prayer," Hester announced and they all said it, Selden and Mike pretending that
they knew it, but repeating all the words a little after the
others. Who was laughing? The mourners would not lift their
heads to see. Loie abandoned the carriage of funeral guests
once and for all to stagger after a bee. Selden needed to blow
his nose.

"Now we have to sing a hymn," said Hester. "We all have
to sing 'Rock of Ages.'" Most of them were able to sing it,
those who did not remember the words at least mumbling
away at the tune. But now there was no doubt that it was
Mike who was laughing; he could not help it any more than
Selden could help having his nose run, but it was annoying,
especially as he had lost his two front teeth and looked awful.

Then came the burial. Alida and Germian were packed
away in their boxes, and Hester sprinkled the open graves

with the ashes she had gathered from the ash trays in the house.

"I know a funeral poem," said Selden unexpectedly, and before anyone could stop him he recited it:

> "Ashes to ashes,
> Fire to fire,
> Show me a woman
> That isn't a liar."

Mike was uncontrollable after that, and Uncle Gill was almost as bad. "*Sel*-den!" said his mother, but even she was smiling.

"Boys ruin everything. Shut up, Selden," said Dody. "Go on, Hester; don't pay any attention."

They covered the coffins with soft earth, patted it into shape, and set the two kindling-wood crosses in place. They ornamented the graves with dolls' teapots full of violets and scillas and sprinkled apple petals on them, and the funeral was over. Aunt Perley lighted a cigarette and hooked her arm in Uncle Gill's. The children's mother captured Loie, picked her up, and blew into her neck, and Loie bleated and laughed and kicked out her legs.

Dody was a funny girl. She had sent Germian off to eternity with only jelly beans and begrudged the golden cover; yet now a struggle with tears was visible on her face.

"I don't like it," she said. "I want her back."

"Dig her up again then," suggested Mike.

"Mike, she can't!" said Hester. "Germian is dead! She has to stay buried."

"But I want her back!" said Dody, and her voice wobbled.

"Tomorrow you'll feel different. You must be brave. You must bear up. Come on and play Squat Tag."

They played Squat Tag and Red Light and Statues and climbed the more dangerous trees, and then they went down to the pasture to look at the colt, and ended up, late in the afternoon, at the barn, where all the cows were being milked, sighing and switching and shifting their feet. The old hay in the loft above bellied out like a cloud; they climbed up the ladder and into the hay, and rolled there and sneezed and buried each other, and at last lay quietly for a little, and all in a row, resting. The sunrays that came through the cracks looked solid, fuming with motes. The air smelled of dung and last year's meadows. The sounds were the sizzle of milk in the pail, deep, juicy chewing, and the twitter of swallows in the rafters. Dody did not mention Germian again.

In the evening, after supper, they played other games: Giant Steps and Still Pond No More Moving, and All-ee, All-ee In-free. The swallows came out in the evening air and flew high up, in patches; then came the bats, whose flying was like scissors cutting fancy patterns. The sun went down, though leaving light behind it, and the little bit that was left over from the winter came up out of the ground in cold and shadows.

Selden and Mike ran wild; they chased each other between the trees and made loud noises and tripped up the girls. It took their father to herd them in.

The living room smelled close of cigarette smoke; radio voices gabbled against the other grown-up ones. Hester and Dody got down by the cat basket to play with the kittens, which were just beginning to stagger. The mother cat stared into space with eyes like melted butter; now and then she gave one of her offspring, or herself, a lick, without thinking about it.

Hester and Dody were smart; they stayed down low and quiet. The grown people were arguing about politics, and the girls knew that this argument was woven above their heads like the stuff of a tent; they could shelter under it, if they kept still, till long past bedtime. But the boys had not caught on, of course; they kept jumping up and making noises and pretending to shoot each other until, naturally, the attention of the adults was diverted to them.

"My soul, it's after nine o'clock!"

Mike and Selden went up first; it was only right that they should. Going by their door fifteen minutes later Hester could see Selden climbing the little ladder to his roost on top of the double-decker bed. Mike was lying on its lower shelf aiming his Pat Perkins Planet gun at the electric light bulb. Dody whispered good night at her own door because Loie slept in the same room with her.

"Good night, sweet dreams. I'll wake you up early and we'll go out without the boys to bother us."

Hester went on to the room where she was staying, a little place that once had been the sewing room. She undressed slowly and got into bed. Not much later she heard Dody's father and mother coming up the stairs and yawning together, and pretty soon Aunt Perley and Uncle Gill. The doors closed one by one, but it was a long time before the house was still; people walked about as they undressed; a man's loud yawn came through partitions, someone laughed, shoes dropped, water rushed through the bathroom pipes. The double-decker bed in the boys' room creaked like a catboat when anyone turned over, and a continuous murmur came from within it. There was furious adult hiss: "Boys! Be still!" Hester heard a final giggle, a final snort and scuffle, and all was quiet in that quarter, but for a while the other voices sighed and babbled, yawned and queried. Loie cried out sharply, and Dody's voice said drowsily, "It's nothing but a dream, baby; you go back to sleep."

Hester always had a room to herself, wherever she was. At home it was next to Mother's, and even when Mother was out at night the smell of her perfume came in a current from the dressing table in her room right to the bed where Hester slept. Sometimes if she had a bad dream and Mother was still out she would go and find Aggie in her little tousled room behind the kitchen. At Father's house she had a room next to the one where Father slept with Martha, her stepmother. She could hear their voices in the night sometimes, never their words; they could have heard her easily, too, but when she had bad dreams she did not call them.

She lay on her back with her eyes wide open like Alida's, until the dark became less dark, the way it always does, and she could see the furniture and her clothes hung over the rocking chair. There was moonlight, bars and spears of it, in the looking glass above the bureau. Someone was snoring somewhere—a man, of course—but otherwise the house was silent. Everyone was sleeping; all of them, even Dody, had gone away to that far place and left her.

After a long time Hester got out of bed and opened her door. It was so quiet between the snores that she could hear the kitchen clock. She crept along the hall and down the stairs, which creaked in several different keys, but woke nobody. The living room was dim and silent; she had forgotten about the cats in their basket and almost stepped on them in the dark—a warm, living, shapeless, breathing bundle, horrible at this moment! Frightening! Like a huge woolly caterpillar with a lot of heads. Hester got past them to the front door and opened it.

Moonlight is never as light as they say it is in books: it is only half-light; it is queer. The valley that she knew well by day was deeper now and longer, and the trees lay on it in soft hummocks, looking like the cats in the basket, furry, soft, alive. Except for the apple trees—they were lighted up like clouds, and they smelled very still and strong of blossoms. A dog a mile away barked out and was answered by one farther on; the grass was wet and icy underfoot. Terror was everywhere; it lay still and perfumed in the white apple flowers, it lay in inky shadow under every tree, it beamed from the bright sky, was poured in waves out of the moon itself. Hester's heart thudded in her chest like a little man running; it shook her body and squeezed her breath, but she waded on through the new, soaked grass to the dark patch beneath the funeral tree. She had not brought anything to dig with so she used her hands and pretty soon she had the box. It was wet, drenched through already, soft as flannel, but Alida, inside it, was intact, smelling only a little more of glue than usual, as she always did when she got damp.

Hester wiped her hands off on the grass and holding Alida against her ribs ran back to the house, into the living room, past the terrible cats, up the staircase, and into her room. She sat for a while on the edge of her bed till the little man in her chest stopped running and she didn't notice her breathing any more, and then she got under the covers and waited for her feet to get warm.

Alida lay beside her, her head on the same pillow, but now the moonlight was not dim enough. Hester could see the open eyes staring at the ceiling with small hard sparks of light in them, like rhinestones.

"It's nothing but a dream, baby; you go back to sleep," she said softly, but the bright eyes continued to bother her for some reason, and after a while she got up and found a piece of Kleenex to put over them as a blindfold. "Now you'll be able to go to sleep," she whispered to Alida, and pretty soon she was asleep herself.

Fair
Exchange

Sylvia Howard and her friend Jane Pemberton were walking on the beach looking for bits of ocean glass. It was a mild November day with a pewter-colored sky and very little wind. The sea tolled calmly as it broke and spread its fans of foam along the tidemark.

"Here's a blue one," said Jane, stooping. "Sapphire blue. You can use this, can't you?"

Sylvia took the piece of glass. She had a bowl full of these smoothed, rounded fragments in her living room, and sometimes when she was alone she would finger them and count them over, as if they were really the jewels they resembled.

"Perfect," she said, holding it up to the mild light. "Gem quality, not a crack or a sharp edge, a real cabochon. From a milk of magnesia bottle, no doubt."

"Or Bromo Seltzer," said Jane pensively. She was spending a few days with her friend and they had sat up far into the night, talking and sipping highballs.

Close to the sea a covey of sandpipers traveled a parallel course, their little legs snipping at the foam like embroidery scissors. Farther up the beach the large winter gulls were standing in profile, pointed toward the sea. As the two women drew near, the gulls lumbered into the air and settled farther on. Soon they would do this again, and then again.

"What masculine birds they are," said Sylvia. "A seagull to me is always 'he.' I never think about there being seagull hens."

Jane did not answer. She was looking at a boarded-up house which rose sharply beyond the dunes.

"Now, those people. The Paulsons (I haven't thought of that name in five years), what has happened to them?"

"Oh, didn't you know? They broke up the year after you stopped coming here. It was the major scandal that summer. It seems he was having an affair with the receptionist at Atlantic Lodge. Had been, for a long time. And then *she*—you remember she was rather pretty? Well, she took a course in anthropology and wound up married to a Turk. They live in Hartford."

"Heavens, this *place*," said Jane. "Things happen to people so. Do you suppose there's something the matter with it? Charged air of some kind? Radium deposits in the earth?"

"Things happen to people everywhere," Sylvia said. "All lives are strange."

"No, but Sylvia. Since last night I've heard about three divorces; four, now, with the Paulsons. And there was the Fine girl's breakdown, and Tony Jackson's, and old Mrs. Craddock turning out to be a secret drinker. (Mrs. *Craddock*, that Whistler's Mother; I still can't believe it.) And then Leila Gebney and the fishman, and Dr. Archibald's conversion, and Mary Totter writing that book. Now, you must admit . . . And all of it happening, or at least all of it coming to light, only in the last five years; just in this one little summer community."

"This one little summer community is a microcosm. We can observe each other more easily, that's all. Things happen to people everywhere, the strangest things."

"My life seems reasonable enough," said Jane. "Suburban housewife and mother. Same husband for fourteen years. Montclair in the winters and Nantucket in the summers."

"Yes, but Jane, think: What made you stop coming *here* in the summer?"

Jane looked discomfited. "Oh, that. But I got all over it. I ran into him last year at the theater, and I thought, How *could* I have! And besides," she said, rallying, "it was in this place that it happened. There *is* something about this place."

They walked on in silence. And Jane's other adventures in other places, Sylvia thought. Her need of secrets, her dread of age; but she was fond of her friend and said no more.

A break in the dunes showed them a view of land: the fields tamped down by the season and dotted with gulls, trees bare of leaf, and a little white house with a black hedge all around it.

"Whitney Parmenter's house," said Jane, with some relief. "Does he still stay here the year round? I'm sure *he's* just the same, at least. Nothing ever happened to Whitney."

"He died, though," Sylvia said.

"He *did?* I never heard! Well, there you are."

"Oh, Jane. Death isn't partial to regions."

"But that he died. It's so unlike him somehow. Anything so real happening to him, I mean. His whole life seemed to be the Social Register and his garden and those Lowestoft muffin dishes that nobody ever saw."

"I did once. He finally did get around to having a party one summer; just one, and I know it caused him pain. He had rum cocktails and they ran out."

"What was the house like?"

"Perfect of its kind. A bachelor's nest, of course. A great many valuable little objects on tables. Piranesi prints and the Lowestoft and so on . . . Oh, people always did talk about the way he went to everything and never entertained, himself. But of course he was in an unassailable position, being the only single man in miles."

"Do you remember how he always knew who everybody was, or had been? 'She was a Pratt,' he'd say, or 'She was a Kissam,' just as if he were classifying beetles. Well, at least there's one that escaped the powers of this place. Nothing happened to him but death. I don't think he was even a pansy, do you?"

"He wasn't such an open book as you might imagine, though. I found that out one fall."

"Now, here's another shoeshine box," said Jane. "The

amount of shoe-shining that must go on aboard ship! . . . But tell me about Whitney."

"You know how I love to come here in the autumn," Sylvia said. "Every year when the children are in school I try to sneak a few days off by myself. Everything seems pared down then, reduced to essentials. The houses are closed, the beach is bare, you don't have to fuss with the garden. All you hear is sea, and some leftover crickets in the weeds. Oh, and the geese! Canada geese. The first time I heard them I thought it was a pack of hounds. They don't honk, they bark; they yelp. But the yelping was coming from the sky, and when I looked up there they were with all their necks out and their mouths open.

"So one fall, three years ago it was, I came down here by myself. I'd had a fight with Donald. Nothing serious, you know, just a married fight, and I felt we needed a vacation from each other and *I* needed a vacation from everything. If I could have stepped out of my skin and had a vacation from myself I would have been grateful, but failing that—"

"Oh, I know that feeling so well," said Jane. "To escape for a while into another personality, a larger one. To exist for a few days in the personality of someone like Albert Schweitzer, for instance."

"Well, failing that, a change of place has to do," Sylvia continued firmly. "So down I came on that awful afternoon train that stops at every single station and often in between, nobody knows why, and by the time I got here it was nearly dark. I took the taxi (the car was up for the winter), and I remember standing on the steps watching it drive away as I searched in my bag for the door key. Oh, that sound of ocean! It seemed to smooth my feelings almost at once; that sense of a continuum that nothing else can give so strongly!

"There was a little wind, not much, and the fields were dark around the house. It was very lonely and I loved the loneliness, but I remember that when I finally did get hold of my key and opened the door, I reached for the light switch in a hurry. The house was so still and so dark (the windows were shuttered, of course) and it had that dead, deserted smell of a house shut up, though it had been closed for only five or six weeks at the most. And then I pressed the switch and nothing happened! No light. Well, I give you my word that what I felt amounted to panic. Real panic, I can't imagine why. I ran to the table lamp and tried that but it didn't light either, and I had this unreasonable feeling that something malevolent was at work. That feeling—you know?—that someone, something—oh, worse than a man, worse than a human being—was waiting for me in the darkness, perhaps very close. My first impulse was to grope for the phone and call Charley Berry, but of course the phone had been shut off for the winter. Everybody has at least one little stinginess that he nurses along through life, and turning off the telephone, even before we're out of the house, is Donald's."

"I know what mine is," said Jane. "It's that I never throw away my shoes. My shoe bags are bursting with warped old slippers I'll never wear again. But go on, go on."

"Well, by this time I was really sweating, and I could feel my scalp *creeping*. I got myself into the kitchen by sheer determination and *then* I couldn't find the flashlight we always keep on the window sill. (It turned out that little Donald had taken it to school with him but had neglected to tell me.) And of course I'd put the matches in a canister where the mice couldn't get at them and then I couldn't remember which canister. The racket I made clattering about in the pantry, snatching off metal lids and dropping them, only frightened me more. When I finally did get hold of the matches I couldn't find a candle, and by then I was really beginning to gibber. Also there were no fuses in the utility drawer. Not a fuse. But luckily we had two kerosene lamps left over from one of the hurricanes, and they were still half full. Once I got those lighted I felt better. I found a bottle of whisky in the pantry, too, and I had a little of that. Then I was fine again. You know, peaceful. Nobody calling me, nobody asking me anything or telling me anything. I opened a can of soup and that was my supper, and then I took one of the lamps and went all through the house, looking at everything. The children's rooms with the summer toys, the odds and ends of summer trinkets like these bits of glass and the old limey shells they collect and the sand dollars, seemed—I don't know —seemed *touching.* I had the feeling that a great time had elapsed, as if I were an old, old woman far from my life with my children instead of at the very center of it. And Donald's swimming trunks and his wilted beach shirt hanging on the bathroom door, even they seemed touching. They made me see that our quarrel was nothing. If the damned telephone had been connected I would have called him and told him so. Life, just because of these reminders, these empty reminders of summer, suddenly seemed so little, so fragile, something to be handled so tenderly—"

"Yes, but where does Whitney come in?" said Jane.

"Now, wait." (She really is rather insensitive, Sylvia thought.) "You must let me tell it in my own way. So that night I confess I locked not only the front and back doors, but my own bedroom door, as well. I'd brought the kitchen alarm clock upstairs with me, but it had such a brutal tick, almost a stamping, that I finally smothered it in a drawer with Donald's underwear and summer shirts. Before I got into bed I opened one window and unfastened the shutters. It had turned into a perfect night; the moon was dead full and only a few stars were strong enough to shine against it. I could see the Burnside farm lights far away across the fields, the only lights I saw. The wind had died and the sea had that sound like breathing—not chopped and blurry, not a roar, but that spaced, matched, perfect sound of breathing. I felt simply wonderful, oh, *peaceful;* I read for a while and then went to sleep like a baby.

"So I don't know what time it was when I woke up. I could hear the clock struggling away in the bosom of the bureau drawer, but I didn't get up and take it out; for some reason I didn't feel like making any noise. *Some*thing had wakened me, I knew that. And then as I lay waiting I heard it again, a stirring about outside, a crunching among the dry weeds. Then a sigh, or a mutter. Oh, Jane! The first fear, the fear of the dark house sprang up all over again. But I managed to crawl over to the window and look out, and there in the moonlight, in my garden, there *was* somebody, a man. I couldn't see what he was doing; he seemed just to be standing there.

"I was so terrified that the darkness began to sparkle all around me and my ears sang. I simply could not stand still and endure the fear; if I had been watching a murderer I would have had to call out and tell him to kill me quickly. Any action, no matter how outrageous, would have been better than that suspense."

"So you called out?"

"So I croaked out. 'Who is there!' I croaked. Oh, I frightened him, too, I can tell you! He was so startled that he groaned, and then he said my name. 'What are you *doing* here?' he said, sounding petulant more than anything, and immediately I recognized that reedy voice. 'Whitney Parmenter!' I said. I was ready to cry with relief. 'I came out here to give Donald a vacation from me.' (I thought it sounded more suitable to put it that way to him.) 'But what on earth are *you* doing out *there?*' And he said, 'I couldn't sleep. I have insomnia lately, and sometimes it helps me to go out for a walk.' Then he sort of cleared his throat and said, 'Often I walk over here.'

"I don't know why I didn't think that was odd at the time, but I didn't. 'Come on in and have a drink,' I said. 'Donald overlooked a bottle of Scotch.'

"I grabbed Donald's old summer bathrobe out of the closet and put it on—you can imagine how glamorous, like an ulster —and I slapped on some lipstick and ran a comb through my hair. After all, it was only Whitney. Then I took the lamp and ran downstairs and opened the door.

" 'No lights?' he said, and I explained.

" 'Never mind; the lamplight is becoming to you,' he said.

It doesn't sound exactly like a compliment, now I think it over. *He* looked just the same, pale and tall and plump with that bulge of forehead and the tiny straight mouth. But he was untidy and that was unusual. (You remember all those madras shirts and the silk scarves folded in at the neck?) The pockets of his jacket sagged as if they had stones in them, and there was dirt on both the knees of his trousers. He told me that he had fallen coming across the Burnsides' potato field. 'Caught my foot in a chuck hole,' he said, 'and went down as if I were praying.'

"It was queer about Whitney that night. You remember how he was. All winter long one never gave him a thought, and then the summer would come and you'd see him on the beach or someplace and think, Oh, yes, Whitney Parmenter. He came in handy if you had a single woman for the weekend or dinner. He wasn't a man exactly, at least in any potentially promising sense, but neither was he another *woman,* and he always talked nicely, filled up the pauses with those educated platitudes: 'I can't admire what Dali paints, but he certainly is a marvelous technician,' and that sort of thing. But this night he seemed to be putting himself out for me, and I had never liked him so much. We gossiped and laughed, and we had one drink and then another, and then he got up to go—I don't know what time it was, but late—and I stood up, too, and suddenly he put his arms around me and kissed me."

"Whitney *Parmenter!*" cried Jane.

"I know. I was so shocked that I kissed him back. Well, I mean it would have been so rude not to."

"But Whitney *Parmenter,*" said Jane.

"And then I stammered something awful, like 'We mustn't,' and gently pushed him away, and he let go of me at once, almost—I thought almost with relief.

"I propelled him to the door somehow, clucking and blushing, and got it open, and there was the night, huge and starry and impersonal, and the sea beating cold on the beaches. . . . And Whitney took my hand and said, 'Can't you guess? Can't you guess why I cross the fields at night to stand beside your house?' And then he gave a sort of ghastly, unsuitable laugh, as though he were rehearsing a scene, and had just heard how badly he'd read the line."

"But Whitney *Parmenter,*" Jane said for the third time. It sounded monotonous, like the call of a bird.

"That's what I thought. I can't tell you how I felt. Embarrassed; flattered, maybe, but uncomfortable above all. I don't know what I said. I think I thanked him. I think I touched his shoulder. And then he was gone, his bald head twinkling through the darkness, and I closed the door and bolted it.

"I went home the next day. I was afraid he might come back and be difficult, but really I need not have worried. I never did see him again, and as the winter went by I used to think about that night now and then, and laugh to myself. But also I redesigned Whitney in my memory a little bit so that I felt rather pleased and flattered, too, and when I heard in May that he'd died of a stroke I really felt a twinge of regret. A real twinge."

"That paper doll of a man!" Jane said. "I can't get over it."

Above their heads nine swans flew by in single file. Between the sound of waves there was a sound of wings.

"Yeats calls that noise 'the bell-beat of their wings.' But I don't think it's anything like bells, do you?" said Jane.

"Donald says it's like the bending of musical saws. But that would never do for poetry." Sylvia stooped for a fragment, appraised it absently; discarded it. "Jane, do you remember my Lycoris Squamigera? It bloomed every August."

"Your what?"

"The Lycoris—the resurrection lilies, *you* know."

"You mean those lovely ghostly pink things that grew in a rank by the wall?"

"Yes, those. Well, that spring only two or three came up. Winter-killed, Donald said; I should have taken the bulbs up. He likes to make me feel guilty about things like that (you know how they are, and he never does *any* gardening himself). I was sad; I loved those flowers.

"And then one day in August I went for a walk alone and found myself approaching Whitney's little house. It had a For Sale sign out in front, and on an impulse of curiosity and maybe—I admit it—from a feeling of sentiment, I walked up to the house and around it to the back where his garden was. I had never seen the garden; it was all walled in by that great hedge. So I turned the corner briskly and stopped dead, because *there,* in a perfect profusion of bloom, were my resurrection lilies. All of them."

"Now, how could you know they were yours?"

"Oh, everything pointed to it. Clear as day. *I* didn't have them, after all. And I remembered the earth on Whitney's trouser knees, the sagging pockets, the stealth. . . . But the conclusive proof was the fact that Lucilla Davis's three Jillian Wallace lilies were right there beside them, and in fine fettle. *She* thought mosaic or the mice had done for them, and she was really grieved, because besides being beautiful they'd cost her fifteen dollars apiece!

"However, there they all were, in splendid health, nodding and prancing in the sunny air. If flowers could laugh, those flowers were laughing."

"And so the confession of attachment and the kiss were simply—"

"Exactly," said Sylvia, and because she was fond of her friend she did not resent the trace of feminine malice in her laughter. Indeed, she had made her a present of it.

"Oh, but Whitney Parmenter!" Jane cried, for the last time. Hearty laughter always caused her eyes to water and now she wiped her tears away contentedly. "Oh, it must be this place. It forces people into freakish ways."

"No, Jane. All people are strange," Sylvia insisted. "Think of the wishes we have. Haven't you ever wished anyone dead? Someone you loved, even? Haven't you ever imagined theft or murder or suicide? Or crazy seduction scenes? And think of our dreams at night! No, the wonder is we're not more freakish than we are." She stooped again. "Now, here's an emerald. Pure emerald from a White Rock bottle. Gem quality."

Jane glanced perfunctorily at the bit of green on Sylvia's palm, and then, as if the glass chip had been a goal of some sort, the two women turned on a common impulse and started walking back along the beach.

A Little
Short
of
the
Record

The guide's name was Captain Len Baker. For the first hour or two the people in his fishing parties called him Captain Baker, but pretty soon they called him Len though he went on calling them Mr. or Mrs. Whatever-it-was.

Gregg had been calling him Len all morning but Celia still called him Captain, or just "you." They had been out on the flats since eight o'clock stalking bonefish, and so far had had no luck though several times they had seen little regattas of silver triangles as the fish "tailed" in the shallows.

"They feed like that, snoot down," Len said. "Anyways, they do in the warm weather. In winter seems like they don't even want to get their tail ends out where it's cold."

He stood in the prow of the skiff, poling the boat stern forward; he was a young man, thirty-two or -three, burned to a deep red-brown. He wore dark glasses and a shredded straw hat; around his lips was a circle of white zinc oxide, and as he poled evenly and quietly his trained eyes roved over the flat thin water. If there was anything worth seeing he would see it.

"There's a fesh there," he said. "But it's a country mile away. Over clost by that mangrove bush. Watch."

The mangrove bush, like all its kind, stood up out of the water on a lot of hooped legs. Whatever fish had stirred there was gone now. It was nearing noon, and the water of the keys was a new color. In the early morning it had been milky-blue and brown; later it had looked yellow, and close by it still looked yellow but in the distance it was green as jade. Pilings from the old railroad trestle stood up in a line between mangrove humps, and every piling was topped with a bird, a pelican or a cormorant, even a gull or two. Some of the cormorants were drying their wings; they held them out, open from the shoulders.

"They remind me of those jackets traveling salesmen hang up in their car windows," Celia remarked.

Gregg said nothing; whimsey bored him. Len said nothing as he had not listened.

The pole dipped quietly into the water, and the boat breathed forward. Reflections of cloud glazed the water with white. They could hear the traffic brushing along the mile-distant highway.

"Nurse shark there to the left," Len said, pointing with the pole; a ragged shadow slipped over the marl and weed, and far out on the shallowest flat a Ward's heron stalked with the villain's step and the fanatic stare of a mad professor.

"Well, where's all the fesh?" said Len, after a long lulled silence. "They oughta be tailin' good. Water's about ten inches, just right. Weather's just right. Might be it's gointa be a storm tonight or tomorrow. They always seem to know, and then they duck down somewheres out of sight. You folks want to eat now?"

"Might as well," Gregg said, taking off his beaked cap and blotting his forehead with a handkerchief. He was an extraordinarily handsome man; his black hair, barely skimmed with gray, rippled back from his brow in deep, perfect waves. In his sun-dark face three things always struck a blow in the solar plexus of any woman who met his direct regard: the even blackness of his eyebrows, the flawless light blue of his eyes, the white, white teeth. As he grew older he grew handsomer, and in this Celia was well aware that she would not be able to keep pace with him much longer.

The guide poled to a little channel between two mangrove

islets. On a silvery old knock-kneed platform there was an assemblage of lobster pots and a dry seine. Len moored the boat there and they sat in the strong light and ate their lunch. It was now the very middle of noon; everything seemed stilled, held in suspension. The old tough birds on the trestle pilings were motionless as gatepost birds.

But in the deep little channel below them, shadows curved and flitted.

"Snapper down there," Len said, through his sandwich. "Big one's a snook. Caught me plenty of good tarpon here, too, after sundown."

Gregg carefully extracted the lettuce from his sandwich and dropped it overboard, where it wagged away slowly on the current.

"Best tarpon I ever got was off the coast of Cuba," he said, without looking at Celia. Then he took a bite, chewed, and swallowed it. "Ninety-seven pounds."

"Man, that's a big fesh!" said Len.

"Sure gave me trouble," Gregg said. "We were fishing off Batabanó when we contacted this baby. Felt as if a pile driver had struck. I swear. And then the fun began; it took me five and a half hours—*five and a half hours*—to boat the bastard, and every time I got feeling like I might conk out the skipper would douse me with a pail of sea water. After a while the other fishing craft around quit what they were doing and closed in to watch the circus, and when we finally boated this baby they cheered; I'm telling you they really cheered! Ninety-seven pounds."

"Man, that's a big fesh," Len repeated approvingly.

"Don't know if I'd care to meet another one like that one," Gregg said with a laugh.

Celia was silent. The story was not true. The tarpon had been caught by Jates Wellington, a friend of Gregg's whom she disliked and who disliked her. It had taken him three hours to land the fish, not five, and Gregg had told the story so often as happening to himself that he probably believed it by now. It was the same with the story about how he had won a packet at Santa Anita in 1949. Actually he had lost a packet. And there was the account of his excellent advice to the Secretary of Defense, and how this advice had been praised and acted upon, when in reality he had once sent such a letter to the Secretary and it had never been acknowledged.

When he told these harmless, ornamental lies Celia hated and despised her husband. The fact that he told them in front of her, aware that she knew they were false yet would permit them, both hurt and shamed her. Then began the argument or the explanation to that imaginary third person whose all-seeing eye could never be deceived. Where is your integrity? inquired this observer. There was no real reply. There were only glimpses, concessions, memories: Gregg teaching Stevie to pitch a ball; sitting up with a colicky baby in the night; his tact and patience with the children in their adolescence (more than she herself could give); his silent fortitude long ago when he had lost his job; his occasional gay drunkenness at parties. There was the way he looked, and there was their bed. Who can stand like a lighthouse, immovable throughout a marriage, glaring toward integrity?

"If you've finished congratulating yourself about that tarpon for the thousandth time, maybe we could continue our search for these measly little bonefish," said Celia sharply.

Gregg laughed. By ignoring her anger he avoided the danger of bringing its cause into the open; he was very good at that. But Celia could feel a sudden startled attention in the attitude of the guide.

The light of early afternoon was flat and all encompassing and seemed as it always did to her, the only light of truth; hope and illusion were equally bleached away with other tender colors. The thin waste of water, the gentle movement of the boat, the figure at their backs poling them forward, all gave the scene a flat, timeless quality as if this moment separated from the context of their lives might last forever.

"Was Charon old or young?" said Celia, too dazed with light to keep her anger. "I can't remember. I think he had a beard."

"Well, it's a question. How old *is* an immortal?" Gregg's firm hand came down on her dry nervous one.

The guide drove his pole deep into the marl and lashed the painter to it. Swiftly and quietly he baited the hooks.

"Where?" inquired Gregg. "I don't spot them."

"Shh, you gotta be *quiet*," whispered Len. "They're shy. I seen them scatter for a butterfly's shadow. Over there. Yonder."

In the patched water to the stern they could see a quirk, a tipped sail flashing like mirror, a triangle, a splash. There was another; two, three, many of them.

Line hissed through the air, the bait made a tiny splash far away. "Here, give this to the missis," whispered Len. She took the rod, warm from the sun, and held it tensely. Gregg's line curved to the left and a few yards away from hers. The little sails, capricious, turned listing and flashing, approached the bait, left it, came back. Celia's heart rolled over in her chest.

Gregg's bait was hit first. She could feel his sudden startled wince; the jar of the boat as he whipped his rod back fiercely. "Got one!" He stood up unsteadily and his cap fell onto the floor. The rod in his hands arched like a bow, and the line was drawn straight, straight as a wire . . . and then it slackened, tossed loosely in the wind.

"I lost it," he said despairingly.

"You didn't set the hook right, sir," Len said, with patience. "See, you have to let them take it in their mouth, feel it around, kind of taste it and start to go off with it; *then* set it. They got superstitious mouths, those fesh. I thought you knew."

"Goddamn," said Gregg.

"Well, he's not the only fesh on these keys. Reel in now, sir, I would. There's some after the missis' bait still."

Celia's heart rolled over again. She felt excitement out of all proportion to the cause, and was close to prayer. She watched the little tails turning and tipping, heard the faint flicker of their movement, and when she felt the first tentative, testing of the bait disciplined herself to wait the short moment before the assertive pull, the grab. Then she jerked the rod up.

Line whistled from the reel.

"Just let him run, just let him run," sang Len gently, as if these were words to a lullaby.

Far away the water rose up in a wing as the line cut it, and the fish rushed in a great circle around the boat.

"A good seventy-five yards he's took," Len said. "Now, missis, pump him e-easy and start to reel as you go down."

"Good girl, Celie," said Gregg. *"You're* doing it right."

Another thing about him was that he was generous.

Her arm and wrist ached from the pumping and winding, and there was a sore spot on her diaphragm where the rod handle was braced. Every time she brought the fish close enough to see it, dark and fleeting, it would take fright and fly with the line again. Sweat fell from her forehead, and she was in real pain as she worked, but at last she had it close enough to the boat so that Len could reach out with his net and ladle it from the sea.

"Son! That's a beauty! Go better than ten pounds, I reckon."

"Congratulations, darling," Gregg said, patting her shoulder. As for her, she was trembling, her right arm almost palsied, and she sank to the seat, laughing weakly.

The great fish, armored in silver, lurched and strove in the net; with all its struggle of motion its eye remained unmoving, fixed in a bright hard stare.

Len hooked the fish scale under its gill and held it up.

"Twelve pounds and a little!" he exclaimed. "That's a *fesh.* The *record's* only fourteen, missis! He's hooked good, too. You want to keep him? The weight would justify keepin' him."

She touched the cold, slimed scales with the tip of her finger. "No, let him go."

He put the fish over the side, held it there in the water teasingly for a moment as it struggled in his hands.

"Go on, then," he said. "Go tell the folks."

Off went the shadow, darting and swerving, safe and digni-
fied in its element.

The afternoon wore on slowly; there were no more fish.
Celia sat quietly, secretly reliving and reliving the glory of
her catch as though she had really performed a deed of unusual skill and valor.

At five o'clock when they returned to the dock of the fishing
camp they were sun beaten, spent, and yawning.

"Good-by, Len, and thanks."

"You sure caught a beauty, ma'am. Good-by."

"So long, Len, see you next year maybe," said Gregg. "Coming to the bar, darling?"

"No, I think I'll sleep till dinner."

But after her shower she felt refreshed and wide awake and
decided to join him. As she walked along the path from their
cabin to the main building she was aware of a great feeling
of well-being and peace. The sea was now a pure delphinium
blue, and overhead the coconut palms bridled and rustled like
large dry birds.

Len was coming from the boat dock, sunburned, bowlegged,
amiable.

"Come and have a drink with us," said Celia.

"Why, thanks, I'd like to, ma'am. I sure could use a beer."

"Only a beer?"

She thought of the occupants of the bar with whom she and
Gregg had become familiar in the past two nights after their
days of Gulf fishing. There was the elderly man whose face
up to his eyebrows was dark and clotted, but above them,
where his hat had been, his great bald head was as pale and
polished as an Episcopal bishop's. He had sat drinking zombies
in silence, staring at Celia. There was the woman who had
once been very pretty, still trying to be pretty, still hoping
for a miracle, pursing her pleated lips and twitching at her
scalded curls. As the evening wore on, her voice rambled and
deepened, a flush darkened her cheeks, and there was the
glimmer of gold in her constant laughter. Her husband was
one of the heehawers that collect in the bar of any fishing

camp, and so was the man from Michigan who was obsessed with the idea of Amar'ca and Amar'cans (a narrow band of people holding his own views; the rest were pinkos, eggheads, and slack thinkers).

None of these people went in for beer. And she and Gregg, too, after their rocking, sun-dazzled days, downed their share of harder liquors and went tipsy to bed to sleep the total sleep of children.

"Well, I might make it a dry Martini," said Len, after serious thought. " 'Bout once a year I might take *one*."

"Good."

The screen door sucked shut behind them and they crossed the empty dining room silently on their rubber soles. The waiting tablecloths flapped at the corners, and the rustle of palm fronds sounded, now, like rain.

As they neared the bar they could hear Gregg's voice. "What a fight he gave me!" he was saying, beginning to hee-haw, too, like the others. "Twelve pounds, a little over; not much short of the record! Well, we'd almost given up, nothing nibbled, not even the crabs, and all of a sudden I see these little tails begin to wave, and I wait. I feel this soft little nibble, and I wait. And then when I *strike* it, the line spins off the reel so fast it smokes! I swear. Seventy-five yards before I could draw a breath—"

Automatically Celia and Len had stopped short of the swinging door.

"Look, Mrs. Hanson," said Len in a low voice. "I gotta go home. My wife, I just remembered, she's got her aunt comin' to supper and I gotta get back. She'll have everything fixed."

"Oh. I see. Not time for even one?" But there was no persuasion in her words.

"With her aunt there already, prob'ly? . . . Oh, no, look, ma'am, if I went in there now I'd just get into an argument. Into a fight, I reckon. Heck, it was you caught that fesh; we all know that. I better go."

"All right, Len, I understand. But Len—"

"Ma'am?"

"Do me a favor and don't talk about it, will you? Leave it the way he says it was."

She watched the esteem ebb from his face.

"If that's the way you want it, ma'am."

"Yes. Thank you."

When he had gone she pushed open the louvered door and went over to the bar beside Gregg.

"Why, Celie, I thought you were asleep." His look was startled, even alarmed. Perhaps this time—

"Your hubby's just been telling us about the whopper he caught today," said the former beauty, her hand cupped lovingly around her glass.

"Whopper is right," said Celia smoothly. "Yes, wasn't he fortunate?"

The bartender placed his hands on the bar before her; his forearms, below his immaculate, rolled-up sleeves, were tattooed. On the right arm there was a blue and red picture of a girl in a bikini; on his left there was the bleeding heart of Jesus and a cross.

Celia fixed her eyes on the girl in the bikini, and said: "Give me a Martini, please, Lou. Very dry." (When had she absorbed the fact that his name was Lou?)

"Darling!" said Gregg, his voice solicitous with guilt. "You know you never drink Martinis! You know you can't, darling."

"Make it a double, Lou," said Celia. "I'm drinking for a friend."

The
Riddle
of
the
Fly

Long ago, when our eldest
son was still a little boy, my husband and I rented a house in
West Twelfth Street. It was the first in a row of red-brick
houses, all alike, but ours was distinguished from the others
by the wrought-iron pineapples on the newel posts of the
stoop railings, and by a never-say-die ailanthus tree that grew
out from the side of the front steps with no visible means of
nourishment but mortar.

The house was light and pleasant. There was room for
everyone, and since it had been built more than a century
before, it was beautiful as well as sturdy.

On the top floor, in the boy's room, there were still two of
the original twelve-paned windows, set low because the ceiling was low. These windows faced south; the sun came in
in the mornings and lay on the floor in two rugs of cross-
barred light. There in the sunshine the boy could fight his toy
wars, build block cities, lie on his stomach to draw. From the
windows he would see many turning sunshades of ailanthus
leaves in spring, many quivering blunt twigs in wintertime.
Somewhere in those back yards a single starling lived the
year round; its lewd whistle could be heard even on January
mornings.

One Saturday when I was trying to impose some sort of
order on his room, the boy looked up from his play and

pointed to the left window. "There's writing on that window-pane, Mummy. What does it say?"

"Writing?" I went to look. I had to bend down to see it, but there in a corner of one of the panes a little phrase had been written long ago, scraped onto the glass in an elegant small hand. It was still legible, though dimmed by time and many washings. "Someone must have written it with a diamond," I said.

"A diamond?" The boy scrambled to his feet and came to look again. "What does it say, though?"

"It's Latin. An ancient language. It says, *Habet et musca splenem.*"

"What's that mean?"

"I don't know," I confessed. "All I know is that *et* means *and*. Someone will be able to tell us, though."

But no one could. I was surprised that my more educated friends were nearly as much at a loss as I was. One of them said that he thought the word *musca* meant housefly. Another wrote a note about it to a friend in the Department of Classics at Yale and received in reply (also written in a small elegant hand, but in a twentieth-century one) a letter which said, in part, "The words mean 'the fly too has a spleen,' or 'even the fly has a spleen,' but without any context it is very hard to say what the possessor of the diamond had in mind. The line is not metrical and so is not a quotation from the poets. It's not from Pliny the Elder's *Natural History,* which is the most obvious prose source I can think of. A hundred and fifty years from now when the *Thesaurus Linguae Latinae* has got to S it may be possible to locate the quotation (if it is one). Until then I am not very sanguine.

"In antiquity the spleen seems to have been connected not with anger but with laughter. If the anonymous author knew that, he may have meant, 'Even a fly has a sense of humor.' If he did not, he may have meant 'Even a fly can get mad' (the turning-worm motif). Neither observation has much to recommend it scientifically, but writing on a window is more characteristic of a romanticist than a scientist anyway."

I thought about this puzzle often. The handwriting, sloped and old-fashioned, had been there a long time; its style indicated that it was a product of the middle nineteenth century. But who had taken the trouble to write it there? And why?

This room, small, and at the top and rear of the house, was the kind which in a private dwelling would have been consigned to servants, or in a boarding house to the poorest tenants; and it was probably in such quarters that a family eccentric would have been concealed.

It seemed likely, then, that the signer of the glass had been poor, lowly, or despised, or all three. On the other hand, he had been educated. The handwriting showed that as much as the knowledge of Latin. I nearly always thought of the writer as "he," because in those days, somewhere between the forties and eighties, there cannot have been many women, particularly in this country, who were exposed to a classical education.

The only other clue, if it can be called one, came to light when I was looking over some old books in my mother's house. These had belonged to a family connection who had been Collector of the Port of New York during Lincoln's administration, and most of them were ponderous law books, but there was, as well, a volume of *Useful Greek and Latin Phrases,* and in this I found what I was looking for: *"Habet et musca splenem:* Even a fly has wrath." There was no allusion to mirth, nor to the source of the phrase itself, so that all this discovery provided was the likelihood that the phrase was better known a hundred years ago than it is now.

No further clue has ever come to light, but I have often thought about this riddle, and have invented some highly unlikely answers to explain it. Three of these follow.

Stella

The snow, which had been falling all night long, stopped a little after daybreak. It was several inches deep, and as there was no wind to disarrange it the branches of the trees had thick sleeves of white, and on each sill the flakes lay so light and dry on one another that Stella could even see their shapes if she leaned close and tipped her head right. Each one was fancier than a Valentine, fancier than a lace doily or a rose window. And the touches that were added! Those no mortal mind could have imagined! What caused nature to exert such infinite fancies of geometry on water drops? "God" was the easy answer people gave. But that no longer answered anything for her: everyone's magician-uncle sitting in the sky drawing up the patterns of creation? No, something far better and stronger than that was at work!

She tried to think when she had last seen snow. She could remember snowy days in her childhood, and later at the convent, but not after that. Time, as other people know it, had only recently been returned to her. Before that she knew she had lived for a period without it, in a dream she never tried nor wanted to remember, though often it muttered its threats of memory, like the distant thunder one cannot be really sure one hears.

The room she lived in was very pretty and light. The snow's reflection made it even lighter, and she liked that; it seemed unfamiliar, a new room. But she was glad to be where she was in any case, even alone, now that she understood time again as other people did.

And she was not entirely without friends. There was Ames, who brought the coals for her grate. Ames always had a lot to say about the weather; one would not have guessed there was so much to say about it. And he spoke at length, too, about his dog, Prince, an animal of surpassing intelligence, strength, and selflessness. Ames had promised to bring Prince for a visit one day when Aunt Beasley was away.

Effie, who brought Stella's tray at mealtimes, was another friend. She was a tall starchy girl with crinkled red hair and one dimple that looked as if it had been dented into her cheek with a man's thumbnail. Her conversation concerned the variety of suitors who complicated her life. She spoke with scorn and relish, and though they were of an age, Stella listened to her as a small girl listens to a grown-up sister.

Aunt Beasley could not be called a friend, exactly, though she had played the role of Providence for Stella; one splendid, rescuing act she had accomplished, and that was enough. No trimmings of sympathy or interest were to follow.

In the yard beyond Aunt Beasley's, two children came out to use the snow. Stella watched with interest as they tossed the feathery white stuff, molded it in their hands, threw it at each other; she laughed when they laughed, felt herself a member of the game.

There was a single rap at the door. "Good morning, miss," said Effie, opening the door with one hand, and holding the tray against her hip with the other. "It snowed," she volunteered, nodding toward the window.

"Yes, indeed it did. Good morning, Effie."

"There. Now eat your breakfast while it's hot, miss. I made the porridge myself today. There's none of Norah's lumps in it. You should try to eat more, miss. *She* should let you go outdoors a little; it would give you an appetite."

"Perhaps she will quite soon, Effie." But Stella dreaded the thought. To venture out into the loud, bare daylight of the street? Oh, never. Let it be never!

"She's going wild downstairs this morning," said Effie, with pleasure.

"Aunt Beasley?"

"Yes, Miss Beasley. Oh, she's wild! She's lost a diamond from her diamond ring. Well, it's just gone! Disappeared. Nothing there but the little empty claw. If the other ones, the bigger ones, wasn't there I think she'd think one of us had stole it. Pried it out and stole it. I think that's what she'd *like* to think! Oh, she's turned the house upside down. Went through the laundry hamper; even got Ames to sift the ashes!"

"Perhaps it will still turn up," said Stella, pouring out her tea.

Effie moved about the room, talking, twitching things to rights, pausing to look out of the window.

"Snow is for children, but, oh, the poor horses," she said perfunctorily. "He asked me last night again, miss," she added, turning from the window.

"Jem did?"

"Yes. That's the third time. Some say you should count a man's proposals, no matter how many he makes you, as just the one. But I say a proposal is a *proposal,* and now with this third one of Jem's it makes nine I've had already!"

"Nine, Effie!"

"Nine. But I'm not in any hurry. Jem! A plumber's apprentice! What does he think!"

When Effie had left, Stella sat contentedly stirring her tea. A rusty starling whistled on a twig. The children had rolled up a big ball of snow. Perhaps they were going to make a snowman; she hoped they were.

Overhead there was an unexpected sound, a buzzing. She could not believe her ears; now, in January? But there on the ceiling was a fly. Where on earth could it have come from in a month of snow, long after the death knell should have rung for all its kind? It crawled about the ceiling in fits and starts, as though someone were jerking it at random by a tiny wire. Zig, zag, then it flew to the window and buzzed at the pane.

That was a summer sound. Stella thought of Sister Mary Guglielma at the beehives taking out honey trays, while she and the other girls cowered among the apple trees, watching and squealing.

"Craven! Chickenhearted, all of you!" cried Sister Mary Guglielma, succumbing to the sin of pride, for she was pleased to show her mastery of bees. "There'll be no honey for the bread of cowards!"

In her blue habit, with the bee veil hung over the nun's veil, she resembled a large draped monument as she moved through the orchard grass among the dome-shaped skeps.

Why did I not know that that was bliss? thought Stella, leaning back and closing her eyes. It was so sharp in her mind, even the smell, the smell of August. Windfallen apples, rank grass, heat, the cologne that Mary Ferney was forbidden to use, but used; and her ears remembered the humming of the hives, and the sleek, self-satisfied sound of the warm brook.

"There's a bee on your collar!" cried Mary Ferney, and at that they had all started shrieking and stampeding from the orchard, theatrically panic-stricken. . . .

The fly at the window twanged like a banjo, twisting its legs together.

"Are you hungry, darling? Is that it?" said Stella, feeling love and concern for this curious midwinter visitor. "Shall I prepare a feast for you?"

She put a lump of sugar on a saucer and added a drop of tea to it, since flies are charmed by stickiness, but it took its time about being charmed. It flew here, there, crawled in starts over the mirror, over the wall, tried the teapot which was too hot, and took to the air, flying about the room in long whining ovals. At last, by accident, it discovered the sugar; lighted on it, paused in satisfaction to wring its threads of legs, and fastened itself to the food. Then it ceased, jerked a short distance to the right, jerked a short distance to the left, and returned to the sugar. In the bright light its common little wings were trimmed with iridescence.

What did its restless movements make her think of? Something . . . or someone . . .

All at once, against every wish, she remembered the woman they had called "the Countess" in that place where she had lived for a short time until Aunt Beasley came for her. She saw now that the Countess had been standing in her memory all this time; not even hiding—waiting. There was the raven-black wig, worn crooked, and the fingers, weighted with filmed rings, that plucked and pressed at the folds of a crimson-satin skirt so charted with stains it was like a map of cloth. The Countess's mouth could say terrible and useless things, but it was her eyes one had to remember. They never stopped moving, or hardly ever. Glancing, darting, they twitched here and there—back, forth, up, down, and when at last they came to rest for a moment, it was on something that no one else could see.

"I will not think about the Countess," Stella said, but the quality of her own voice frightened her.

No, think of Sister Mary Guglielma again! Yes. Think of her that day, playing with Léonie's diabolo spool. She was as expert with that as with the bees. How proudly she had walked the gravel drive, showing the girls how she could make the big spool seem alive on its thread, spinning, soaring heavily, lighting heavily, spinning again, never falling.

"You must imagine yourself to be the spool," she had told them. "Put yourself in its place; imagine where you need support; imagine when it is exactly the right time to *fly!*" Up went the spool, turning in the sun.

When Sister Mary Guglielma was tired and sat down on the stone bench to rest, the diabolo spool in the girls' hands, even in Mary Ferney's, turned into a bumpkin, lunging from the thread and rolling away. Sister Mary Guglielma tried to hide the triumph in her manly laughter.

Because of the fly, these memories of the nun were set to a sound of insects; this memory, too, for the tree under which she had sat down to rest had been a lime tree in full flower, vibrating like a wine glass with the hum of bees.

The sun came out suddenly. Stella opened her eyes. The first thing she saw was a piercing glitter on the rug and knew at once it was Aunt Beasley's diamond. Last evening as she sat by the window watching the snow, her aunt had come in, burst in, like the March wind, as usual. "Brooding in the dusk, Stella? *That's* not healthy!" She had seized the chimney from the lamp, and in striking a Lucifer to light it, had also struck her hand against the wall. "Pshaw! What clumsiness!"

Picking up the diamond, Stella had a picture in her mind of her aunt's pleasure. "Stella, dearest, how clever of you!" she was saying as she came forward to embrace her niece.

"Oh, no! Never! It would never be like that! Stop thinking it," cried Stella, thrusting away the fancy as she thrust the diamond into her pocket.

The children's voices were sharp in the yard, and from the muffled street came a scrape, scr-a-a-pe of snow shovels. The fly was making a tour of the window curtain.

Effie knocked at the door, came in with the paper in her hand. "And there's some letters for you, too, miss. What's that, a *fly? This* time of year? Why, the nasty little—"

"*Effie, do not kill it!*"

But Effie, with a swat of the folded paper, had already done so. The fly fell to the sill, dead as a raisin, and Stella burst into tears.

"Why, miss! It wasn't nothing but a fly!"

"But it was alive, Effie. It was alive!"

Astonished and embarrassed, Effie hovered over her, explaining. "They're dirty little pests, miss; *you* know that. Think of what they feed on; why, they're *vermin!* Fie, for crying over such a thing!"

"Oh, Effie, please go away. I'll stop if only you will go!"

"Well, certainly, miss, if that's how you feel." The door closed offendedly, and Stella wept in peace.

Searching in her pocket for her handkerchief her fingers found the diamond a second time. She went to the window and knelt down beside it. The fly lay on its back, its legs crossed as if in prayer.

"Shall I write your epitaph then, darling? For I know the very one to give you!"

It was not easy to do: the little stone kept twisting about in her fingers; twice she dropped it, too. But fortunately it had a sort of point at the end which had been set into the claw, and this was sharp enough to scratch the glass quite nicely. When she had finished, she read what she had written aloud. "Amen," she added, and opened the window. Digging a grave in the snow with her finger, she buried the fly.

The children were nearly finished with their snowman; it had a broom in its arm and a hat on its head, but as yet no face. Stella realized that in her clenched left hand she was still holding the diamond and opened her fingers to see it, obdurate and trivial, on her palm. Thoughtfully she transferred it to her right hand, and then with an abrupt movement she leaned out of the window, and threw it as far as she could, over the back fence into the snow and rhododendrons of the yard beyond. Its fall was so light that the children working on the snowman never noticed it, though it fell close to them.

Having thrown the diamond she could not deny herself the pleasure of throwing something else. First she chose her clock, and then her Bible, and next the silver brush and comb her aunt had given her years ago. Each time she hurled something she shouted to it, "*Go* away! *Fly* away!" and laughed aloud. The two children and the blankfaced snowman stared up at her, and there were sudden faces in the windows opposite.

All at once with a shock of excitement she understood what her own hurling arm had been trying to convey to her; what, in fact, she had been rehearsing.

But when she got one leg over the sill they burst open the door, caught her, and dragged her back.

"Oh, what a spectacle!" hissed Aunt Beasley, gripping Stella to her angry bosom. "For shame, for *shame!* Effie, do you go tell Ames at *once,* to borrow Mr. Taintor's ladder! This shall never happen again! This mortification!"

Later, tied to the bedpost like an animal or a senseless child, Stella saw Ames's face rise above the horizon of the sill.

"What are you going to do, Ames?" she called, so that he might hear her through the glass.

"I'm sorry, miss; I'm sure I truly am. It's orders, though. I'm to nail the shutters down to keep you from flying away, like."

He spoke kindly enough, but he did not quite look at her, and she saw that his opinion of her strangeness had come between their friendship for each other.

It did not take him long to do as he was bidden, and after that, except at mealtimes when someone sat with her, she lived in darkness. They did not trust her with a lamp.

Alfred
and
Theresa

In the garden beyond his there was a pear tree; that was the first thing to light up on April mornings. Even now before day had really begun he could see it showing faintly through the dark and smell the dusty unsentimental odor of its flowers. He had been sitting there beside the open window for a long time, already dressed, but Theresa still lay fast asleep.

At this hour the city's noises were all made one, like the sound in your ear when you cup a hand over it. All nearer noises, except for the coughing, had stopped long ago. That sound came from the house next to the pear-tree house. He had noticed on waking that there was a lighted window there; perhaps the light had been burning all night long. Cough, cough. Such a regular little pair of barks, spaced at intervals of a minute or two, dry and noncommittal. He could not tell if they came from a man or a woman, but he had grown accustomed to them and had the feeling that he and that one coughing were the only two awake in the whole city.

Certainly the house was asleep. Not a sound came from the servants on this floor; not a sound from his wife's room two floors below; and there were no children to wake and cry out in the night.

He thought of his wife, lying in the bed she never left. She had married her illness when she married him, or soon after. The illness was husband, lover, and child to her and she tended it with devotion. The blonde ethereal girl had become a lemony invalid, smiling wanly among her pillows, making requests in her gentle voice; perfectly happy. Perfectly happy . . .

Across the room his eyes could just spell out the shape of Theresa's head against the pillow; at least they could tell the darkness of her hair.

He marveled, now, that though he had encountered her daily at her work for nearly half a year he had hardly noticed her until a week ago. Coming into the kitchen unexpectedly, he had found her there alone bowed above the kettle on the stove.

"What are you doing, Theresa, telling it your prayers?"

She had straightened and turned quickly, laughing. "Oh, no, sir. I'm only taking a bit of steam, the way it will curl me hair for church."

Her face was pink from steam and not from blushing. Dark ringlets dripped on her forehead; her eyes, between black lashes, were an iris-blue. He would never forget her standing there laughing, so beautiful and—not bold, exactly. Free? Flirtatious? For some reason the word "natural" escaped him. Whatever it was, the quality allied with her beauty had set a reckless hope alive in him such as he had not allowed himself to feel in years.

Out of doors the air was altering; day begins before the light does. Once on a beach in Brittany he had watched an incoming tide; far away at first, it had come on and on across the sand wastes, a wide, pale, shallow drive of water, nothing in creation could have stopped it; and that was the way the sound of morning came to the city. It seemed to begin at a great distance, as if all the horses of the town had been released from far-off stables at the same moment. One heard them coming nearer and nearer until the air was ringing with the noise of hoofs and the devil-may-care bang and rattle of dray wheels. There were shouts from the draymen, bells from the river, and the sparrows in the ivy began to assert themselves with a jangle that sounded as though many people were shaking trays full of little tin chips; and with the jangling the light began to rise.

There was something brutal and cheerful about the waking of a city; in Alfred's nature something brutal and cheerful now responded. On an impulse he drew his stickpin from the folds of his cravat. The pin was set with a pointed topaze, and it was with this that he began painstakingly to inscribe a sentence on the window glass, bending close to see in the dim light. He had a feeling which was childish, and he knew it, that during the night just past, and now in writing these words, he was somehow settling accounts—not with his wife, whom he did not dislike—but with events, life, destiny, or some such large, unreasonable adversary.

Among the sparrows' sounds of tin there was a sweet, more formal sound: some migrant country bird. Theresa woke up.

"Whatever are ye doing, sir?"

"You're awake!" He crossed the room and sat down beside her. "My God, you're a beauty even at this hour! It shows how young you are." He lifted the rope of her black hair, tougher and warmer than silk, turning it gently in his hands. "How old are you, Theresa?"

"Nearly twenty, sir. How old are you?"

"Nearly thirty," he said, with a deep sigh.

"Ah, well, ye don't look it at all."

She smiled, stretched, and yawned to the uttermost, the way a child or an animal would. Every tooth was perfect, but that had nothing to do with the matter. She would yawn in the same shameless way when she had not a tooth left in her head.

"Ye'd best be getting on downstairs now, sir."

"Oh, Theresa, not 'sir' when we're alone. Alfred. You must call me Alfred."

"Oh, I could never do it!"

"Ah, why, Theresa? Why not?" He twisted the warm rope in his hands gently, lazily. She smiled, but did not answer.

There was a muffled champing deep in the house.

"Oh, glory! It's Mary shaking down the coals!" Theresa sprang from the bed in her long crumpled nightgown. "Go now, sir! What if they saw you!"

"They won't. I'll be careful. First come here, though. There's something I want you to see." He put his arm around her and drew her to the window.

"Look at that!"

"The pear tree?" She seemed surprised.

"Isn't it a perfect thing?"

"It puts me in mind of a great heap of pot cheese."

"Pot cheese! Theresa! How can you describe it so! It's like snow from the Himalayas, or sea foam. Or a cumulus cloud."

"Like mashed potato, more," said Theresa stubbornly. She was hungry. Then she spied the sentence on the pane. "Is this what ye were at, then? Putting down this bit of writing? And how did ye ever get it onto the glass at all?"

He showed her the pointed topaze on the pin.

"Well, now! And what does it say?"

"It says, 'I love a beautiful Irish girl,'" said Alfred promptly. Theresa could not read her own name, let alone a word of Latin, and knowing this made him feel very tenderly toward her. He took her in his arms.

"Yes, but ye'd best be going now, sir, truly. They've all gone down. Ye'll meet no one on the stair."

"I know; I'll go. I hate to very much, but it will not be for long, I promise."

"No. Good-by, sir."

"Good-by, *Alfred*."

"Good-by, Alfred."

"That's better." At the door he looked back, but she had already turned away. She was standing before the window, looking out. Against the light her linen nightdress was translucent; he could just discern the outline of her figure. Beyond her the pear tree had a bluish cast.

As he went down the stairs he suddenly thought, But that is what I should have written on the glass—the thing I told her! Because it is the truth. He had not bargained for this at all, and it was so surprising to him that he stopped in mid-descent, staring at the changed air. Then he continued down, outwardly quiet and circumspect but inwardly rash with a joy that was all the sharper for its promise of pain.

Theresa remained at the window a moment longer, rubbing her elbows and yawning. As she studied the words on the glass she spoke audibly to herself. She often did this, and when

she was old would be one of those happy crones who go along
the streets laughing at their own jokes.

" 'I love a beautiful Irish girl.' That's what he said it said,
but it does not look as if it said that to me. 'Tis not the right
sort of a shape at all. No, it is not." She put out her finger
to touch the little roughness on the glass, yawning till her
eyes watered.

Cool and solemn came the sound of church bells, blocks
away. Oh, God, six o'clock already! Cook would have her by
the hair!

Hastily she began to dress.

Costigan

Costigan's room was the coldest in the house. Being right up
under the roof, the fireplace drew so well it snatched the heat
straight up the chimney; a foot away from the hearth and
you were chilled through. "That chimney would draw a cat,"
Powers said. And situated as it was, facing south, the room
was bound to be the warmest one in summertime, too. But
what it was like in summer was fortunately no concern of
Costigan's. He would be—he was not certain where, but for
a long while he had had a persistent idea of long, lighted
windows, music, waves breaking on a warm shore. Palm trees
would be chattering in the night wind, and his hand would
fondle a supple waist, all alive within its covering of silk and
whalebone. It did not matter whose waist it was as long as
it was young and slender. Ah, it was hard to wait! All the
harder because the time was near; but he could wait.

He looked into the washstand mirror at his thin monkey's
face, fondled his chin, examined his teeth, then his tongue,
and was just pressing a wave into his black flap of hair when
the bell rang.

No words can describe his loathing for that bell. It tilted
on a question mark of wire above his door, and it was always
interrupting him in his thinking. There never would have
been a right time for it to ring.

"Before I leave I'll take your tongue out," he told the bell, straightened his striped apron, and ran down the stairs. He was very light on his feet.

Birdie was dusting the hall wainscoting. "Where is she?" he said.

"Ye know good and well where she is; where she always is this hour. In the conservatory. She'll be wanting her tea."

"What she's pleased to refer to as her tea, you mean."

He would have liked to take a good pinch of Birdie bending over, but he knew better; her laughter, once freed, was as hard to silence and control as a stampeding flock.

He glanced into the mirror in the parlor hall, turned his head, smiled, always hoping for something better than he found. But money's a great beautifier, he thought to himself.

There was a thick carpet on the drawing-room floor; nothing made a sound as he went through except the lusters on the mantel sconces, which gave a little whinnying of glass. Going through that room was like pressing through an Easter crowd, packed, well dressed, hushed.

The conservatory beyond was lighted through its glass roof by whatever color the day happened to be (today it was gray), and the great creature was seated there in the Turkish chair as usual, in her own small jungle, with the canary birds screaming daintily all around her, and the pale camellias more the color of skin than her own skin was.

"Good morning, Costigan. Where is Powers?"

"Good morning, ma'am. He's temporarily indisposed."

They both knew what that meant, and there were good reasons why she did not care to pursue the subject. "I see. Is it eleven yet, Costigan?"

"It is, ma'am; or lacking five minutes. Would you care to have your tea now?"

"Please. And Costigan—"

"Ma'am?"

"Try to remember to put the decanter on the tray, will you?"

"The rum decanter, ma'am?" When it was his turn to serve her he always allowed a little surprise to show in his voice.

"If you please," she said stiffly, and a touch of color came into her gray cheeks.

He always made her ask for it, too. If she did not ask for it he did not bring it.

As he went down the basement stairs he was thinking of the way everything was opening up for him. Powers, the one possible obstacle, was out of the picture, and by midnight, or long before, *she,* upstairs, would be out of the picture, too. He could not keep from singing a little.

> "How sweet is the sunshine of love on the heart,
>   Its rays stealing down to illume . . ."

The kitchen, as usual, was a cave of crisis. Mrs. Dagle, the cook, found rage a necessity, and causes for it, in her kitchen, were seldom lacking. Her attitude toward the stove, and toward every stove she had ever worked with, was one of watchful animosity, an attitude such as a master might bear toward a treacherous slave. Her attitude toward those she worked with was the same. Jenny, the kitchen maid, sat slumped at the table dolefully peeling potatoes. Her lids were pink, and she sniffled from time to time. As Mrs. Dagle tramped about, the floor shook. She was so fat that when she walked to church holding her prayer book, her free arm did not swing back and forth in the usual way but flung itself around her in a half circle.

"Good morning, love," said Costigan, and she gave the token response which she granted on her better days: a sound with her mouth closed. On the bad days there was not even this.

Her great apron and skirts would furnish a frigate with its sails, thought Costigan. Her shoes had windows in them for her bunions to lean out of, and two slate pencils were stuck into her black, angry-looking hair.

"You put me in mind of an Oriental concubine today, love," Costigan said teasingly. But she would not be teased. It is doubtful if she ever laughed; very few had even seen her smile. "Well, 'tis the ones with the worst tempers make the best cooks. Observe the French," Mr. Powers, the butler, had said more than once. Down here they always called Powers "Mr.," and such is the pressure of environment that even he, Costigan, a former schoolmaster, was infected with awe, with a desire to impress the man, which he knew quite well to be an aspiration without value.

Mrs. Dagle turned on him, red and challenging. "Well, what is it now, then? Where's your tongue? What does she want *now?*"

"It's eleven o'clock, love. She wants her tea."

"Tea! Ha!" Though she did not laugh, Mrs. Dagle had a sort of shout that she employed where others, feeling scorn, might use a laugh.

"Why not take her up the bottle, just? Here! Take it! Take the whole bottle!" She waved the decanter at him.

"There, there, love. Give it here; I'll fix the tray."

She handed it over. One thing about him, he didn't drink. The same could not be said of Mr. Powers, who regular as a clock struck drunkenness once every two months and took to his bed to enjoy it in privacy. He was considerate about it, though, always keeping his singing and soliloquizing pitched to a civil key.

Mrs. Dagle seized the kettle from the stove and took it to the sink where she wielded the pump handle as though punishing a mule. Her fury gave her exercise and in the end would kill her.

"*Drink!*" she cried, slamming the kettle back on the stove so hard that water bolted from the spout. "*Drink* in the parlor! *Drink* in the attic! The house is a scandal. Indeed it is!" But in her voice there was the rich pleasure of indignation justified.

Beyond that the day was slow in passing. Shortly after noon when the sun came out, the wild trilling of the canaries could be heard in every corner of the house. "It makes me feel as if somebody's running a comb over my back. I'd dearly love to set a cat on them!" said Mrs. Dagle, ripping the meat from a drumstick with her square, strong teeth.

To Costigan the shrill vibratos seemed the sound of his own tightening nerves. He was getting as fidgety as a wasp and did not know how he was to endure the rest of the day.

At three o'clock when she, upstairs, had gone to take her nap, already faltering in her steps, Costigan went to the conservatory to water the plants. Birdie was there, polishing leaves with a soft cloth. The sun had moved away and the canaries, exhausted, contented themselves with random chirpings. The conservatory lay in a blue shadow.

"I know one thing, Birdie," said Costigan. "In hell the hour will be permanently three o'clock. Three o'clock post meridiem, in *secula, seculorum*. That means forever and forever, Birdie."

"And how do ye know unless ye've been there already? They say there's no such thing as time down there. There's just eternity."

"Just eternity? And what's the color of eternity? What hour of the day does it resemble? Time will have stopped *somewhere*, will it not?"

"Ah, leave me be, will you? How should I know?"

"It cannot stop nowhere, Birdie. It will have stopped at an hour, a minute, just as a clock stops that never goes again. And I maintain the hour will be three in the afternoon forever, for that's the worst in all the day."

And yet it had not been at three o'clock that the worst had happened to him. It had been at six in the morning when the sky was red as claret and the birds were at their loudest that he had trotted gasping down the road with the stones flying past his ears and the townspeople howling behind.

A windy groan escaped him.

"What ails ye, then? They've not consigned ye to the Bad Place yet," said Birdie good-naturedly. "Best get on with the watering, Costy. Tempus fewgit!" She smiled at him, pleased with herself.

He laid his hand on her shoulder. "You're a good little

pupil, aren't you, Birdie? Fancy you remembering that!" For a moment he felt real regret that after this day he would not see her again.

It was past eleven when the house was settled for the night. *She* had dined alone among her wine glasses, and he, in Mr. Powers' place, had seen that they were never empty. She nearly always dined alone these nights; her children and her friends kept well away. At half past nine when she had tried to conduct prayers she had made such a muddle of it that Jenny was possessed by a storm of giggles and Mrs. Dagle had had to pinch her hard to stop her.

"Come, madam dear, come up to bed," said Nell, her own maid, holding out her hand. She led the great creature tottering and trembling up the stairs, tender as a nurse with a baby.

Costigan in his room was packed and ready, but he waited till he heard the hall clock striking twelve, and then one by one, the great clocks of the city, before he crept from his door.

A reddish glow shone upward through the banisters from the landing light on the floor below. There were no noises in the house but the noises of sleep: Mrs. Dagle's savage snoring, and that of Mr. Powers, which had the rhythmic sound of someone tearing strips of cloth. When Costigan laid his ear to the door of the latter the sound paused as a word of gibberish was spoken, and then resumed. He opened the door gently, removed the key from the lock, closed the door again, locked it from outside, dropped the key into his pocket, and drew a deep breath.

At the girls' door he listened, smiling. Birdie, Nell, Jenny— they were young; they slept like little stones. They were trusting, too, and had not even bothered to take the key inside. He turned it softly in the lock and put it in his pocket with the other.

Mrs. Dagle was not trustful. Her door was both locked and bolted. He got the chair from his room and wedged it under the knob. Fortunately she was a heavy sleeper; one of his duties had been to waken her each morning by pounding at her door.

He walked slowly down the stairs. A red Bohemian glass globe on the landing light gave the hall a dimmed Inferno color, and that was the color of her room, too, as he saw when he eased the door open, for she kept a similar lamp burning on her mantel through the nights. He was prepared for this; Nell had mentioned it more than once. Nor was the room a stranger to him, since it was he who tiptoed in on chilly mornings, when Nell called him to make the fire, and knelt in his striped apron on the hearth, his back to the bed, very quiet, very tactful. Nevertheless, a determined eye can roll half-way round a head and be discreet about it, too. He knew just how she looked there, propped up in her roofed bed like an idol in a wayside shrine, all tufted about with pillows and laces; and none of the frills did a thing to modify the fact of that heavy gray face or soften the harsh troubled sound of her breathing.

But now there was no sound; she lay lost in something deeper than sleep, and not till she emerged into sleep would there be any danger of her waking. The room was close; it smelled of spirits and cologne. The lamp flame stretched, brightened as if widening an eye, and settled. Costigan's big shadow was dead still against the wall; then it moved with him across the room, and as he stooped above the dressing table it stooped above the wainscoting.

He was no longer nervous; on the contrary, he had the feeling, even as he worked, that he was without responsibility, as though he stood at some distance from his own hands and eyes, safe as a member of an audience at a play. But when he caught himself whistling softly he stopped with a chill of superstition. One must always propitiate. But in this case what? Or whom? Who is the patron saint of thieves?

The pearls were in the top tier of the jewel box, blandly gleaming. Their coolness was soothing to his fingertips and he stroked them a moment before pocketing them. In the next tier on the cushioned velvet lay the matched emeralds, necklace, earrings, bracelet. He held the necklace to the light, thinking of the jewel cutters of antiquity who always kept an emerald by them, believing that the contemplation of this stone would heal sore eyes. Looking at them he felt healed himself, he thought, and laughed silently. Next he lifted out the rubies, and the bracelet clasped with rubies, and all the twinkling brooches. He left the cameos with their peevish profiles, and the coral parure, and the other trash. He had the best of it, except for the last thing, and at the thought of this he was returned to his own body, and felt his heart running in his chest.

Crossing the room he stood by the bed and looked down at her. Anyone seeing them would have thought that he was watching her with tender concern. In a way, he was. Her head in its ruffled cap listed against the pillow; her big supply of chin and cheeks was all slid sideways, and her mouth gaped wider at one corner like a buttonhole, but he could not hear her breathing.

Testingly, gingerly, he took her hand in his; it felt next thing to dead, but the great diamond on the third finger winked at him, wide awake. He knew at once that he'd have trouble getting it off, and putting the hand down gently went to the washstand for a cake of soap. When he had soaped the finger the ring came off quite easily. She shifted her head a little, that was all; there was still no sound from her.

He locked that door behind him, too. There was a loud roaring in his ears, and he never remembered going up the stairs.

His room was just as he had left it. The candle seemed to have grown no shorter in its stick; the panes were still black with night. Before he buckled the straps of his valise he took the diamond to the candle to have a better look at it. It was a labyrinth of darting colors, crowded and active, as if the stone were full of little lives. A dart of blue, of green, of blood-red. Claret-red . . . and there was the red morning in his head where it would always be, with the stinging stones and the pack at his heels, and because of them all the shame and struggle and servitude that followed; the "yes, ma'am" and "yes, sir," and polishing other people's shoes and airing their dogs and accepting rebuke like a docile child.

However, he knew the message to leave them now, and he had the pen to write it with.

When he had done he took up his valise, blew out the candle, and left the room. That door he locked behind him, too, and that key went into his pocket with the others. Soon they would all be lying at the bottom of the harbor.

Except for the monotonous sounds of sleep the house was perfectly still. He smiled, thinking of the shouts and rattlings that would soon occur, and was only sorry that he would not be there to hear them for himself; he felt wonderfully exhilarated.

Light as a dancing master, he ran down the stairs.

We left the house in Twelfth Street long ago. For years we have lived in another on Washington Square. This house, in which we occupy three floors, is one of the red-brick Georgian buildings in Old Row.

As I write this, I know that we must leave this house for good in a few days. New York University, which had collected all the others in the Row, has now collected this one. We are told that it is to be made into classrooms and offices.

I look at the big, calm rooms with their marble mantels and mahogany doors. A carefully carved acanthus leaf crests outward from the corner block of each lintel; the ceiling moldings are simple and beautiful. I try to imagine these rooms furnished with water coolers, filing cabinets, blackboards.

At the top of the house, above the stairwell, an oval eye of skylight looks down. The stairs rise toward it in long spiraling ellipses. In the first flight there are twenty-two steps; in the second, eighteen. The graceful regiment of ascending banisters is matched, on the wall, by a graceful regiment of shadows. The handrail has been polished to a high gloss by the whistling breeches of our youngest son; and the family dog, old and blind now, knows the stairs so well that he can race up or down them just as confidently as he did in his sighted youth.

The windows of my bedroom face the park. I wonder how many thousand times I have looked out of them: late at night when the baby was wakeful, or I was; early in the morning when nothing stirred in the air but the pigeons. Clapping down from cornices and branches their wings had the sound of moderate applause.

It is late spring, now; the park is muffled in green, with clots of people showing here and there. But I know how it looks when the trees are bare, and in the snow, and when the leaves are just beginning, and at night, and in the rain.

On certain October afternoons it has an ambery distorted look, as if one were peering at it through a glass of Tokay; and sometimes, though not often, on winter dusks before the lamps go on, I have seen the whole park—trees, plots, paths, people—dyed to the blue of willowware.

Thinking of these windows it has occurred to me that the riddle of the fly may have a very simple answer, after all. Perhaps the words were written on the glass by someone who, for reasons not of his choosing, was forced to leave a place he loved.

The
Morning
of
Diane

All day long in summertime Broderick Atkins, known as Brody, heard the same kind of questions from the people on the beach, the summer people, and gave them the same kind of answers that he always gave and had given for years.

"Do I dare to, Brody?" the women would ask, pointing their toes at the sea. "Is it fiendishly cold? Is the surf heavy?"

"It's a very nice temperature, ma'am," Brody would say, smiling. "Surf's light. I think you'll enjoy it." And pretty soon he'd hear them squeaking as they always did from the first shock of the water.

"What's it going to do, do you think?" the men would ask, dropping down beside him for a moment, nodding their heads at the sky and meaning the weather.

"Well, I think it'll hold fair," or "Looks like rain, maybe; wind's easterly," Brody would answer, as the case might be.

That was about all the conversation he ever had with any of them, except the children. It never bothered him; he liked most of the people in the detached way of one who has seen them come and go, come and go, and felt no pressure of emotion concerning any individual among them. He liked them, but what he loved was the beach, the gauzy air, and the busy sea that he insulted only once a year. In wintertime he thought about the beach on the coldest days, and on the sad sick Sundays when he was coming up through a hangover.

That was what hope meant to him: a bright summer day, the sea, the beach that was his property, the people who needed him; all of that waiting for him every year, year after year.

He had been the lifeguard at the Clam Strand Beach Club for thirty-seven years, a good piece of time in any man's life. He had come to his post a redheaded giant fresh from the wars, and had never missed a working day in all those summers. He had plucked more children away from death, rescued more show-offs, escorted more panicked old ladies out of the surf, than he or anybody else could think of counting. Like the sturdy squat bathhouse which had withstood all storms, he was himself an institution.

Almost no one knew what he did in wintertime. "I don't believe he does *anything*," one frivolous woman contended. "I think they just store him away with the ropes and barrels and beach rakes until the tenth of June, when they take him out and dust him off. Good God, I mean he was here when *Daddy* was a kid!"

The beach changed its contours, altered its dunes, sometimes several times during a season, but essentially it remained the same thing, and the ocean for all its variety remained the same. People do not differ very much from one generation to another, either, though habits and manners change. Brody sometimes thought about it. When he had first come, for instance, the beach had been a far dressier place than now. He himself had worn a bathing suit with knee-length trousers and a tunic that covered his collarbone and had little sleeves. And the young girls who twittered and squealed with identical obedience in every generation had worn stockings and suits with skirts, and since few of them in those days knew how to swim the crawl they arranged their fancy caps on the backs of their heads, leaving large lappets of hair exposed on their cheeks and brows in what were charmlessly called "cootie garages."

Their fathers and grandfathers Brody remembered fondly; old Mr. Elihu, Mr. Butler, Judge Mowrey, and the rest, paunched and stately at the water's edge, all wearing tunicked bathing suits like his own. Many of their undoubting faces were adorned with hair, mustaches or neat imperials. Their wives were kind, respectable women who wore corsets under their bathing dresses and sand shoes on their stockinged feet, and went creaking into the water like firm flounced launches. There, beyond the breakers, they would balance together in a group, some even wearing hats, talking in their cultured city voices as if they had met at church or at a Philharmonic concert. They did this only on the calmest days, of course. When the surf livened up at all they were content to dip in the foam, shriek gently, dab their faces with cold Atlantic water, and then creak back to their knitting and umbrellas.

By now most of those older ones were dead or dispersed, and it was their children who were the middle-aged matrons and businessmen. The matrons no longer wore stockings; they tanned their veined legs just as the young girls did, and the husbands tanned their bare torsos.

Their offspring, the grandchildren of Judge Mowrey and the rest, were the young handsome ones in full possession of the hour. They were the lean, the slender, the quick, with the smooth skins and the bright white teeth; they swam like otters, and took care of their own children. (In the old days there had always been nurses quavering and flapping at the water's edge or settled in a large pelican roost beside the dune.)

But those who remained most the same in all the changing were the children; the weed-haired little boys who refused to come out of the water though indigo-blue and agued, just as their fathers had refused twenty or thirty years ago, and the little girls who, like their mothers before them, sojourned for a while as water rats along with their brothers, hair in strings, tooth braces glaring, at least as shrill and bossy as the boys. . . . There was always a summer when these girls came back looking different, with a new unsettled fatness and the beginnings of breasts; and not long after that, in spite of everything, they became beauties, assured and proud, as if they had accomplished this metamorphosis through will alone.

And then began the courtships of ducking and screaming. . . .

Brody had seen it all, repeated and repeated. First they were babies in the foam, grasping at his great legs as drunkards grasp at lampposts; next they were women raising families and flirting with each other's husbands, and before very long they, too, would be elderly; sagged and mottled, reduced to the passive and conventional by the pressures of time.

Brody himself changed very little, and knew it. He was a huge man, well-built. When he had first come to the job he had had a thick flap of hair the color of tangerine peel, and now the flap was thick but it was white, and the once orange fuzz on his chest and arms was white, too. But his eyes were the same sea-bleached blue they had always been, and his shoulders were as mighty. On his left forearm a rather old-fashioned mermaid posed on her broad-hipped fishtail, as she had since being tattooed there in Marseilles, the summer of '18.

Brody wore a medal of Saint Christopher on a chain around his neck. His mother had given it to him before her death, years ago, and while he was not religious he had a certain superstitious respect for her memory. She had been a devout, uncharitable woman whose talent for devitalizing pleasure amounted to genius.

"Hell, she thought Santa Claus was wicked; she thought a nickel for when your tooth falls out was wicked," Brody said. "Prayers and lickings, lickings and prayers, that's the most I remember about my old lady. I guess she thought she ought to lick me double because my Dad was dead. He died when I was two. Drowned at an Odd Fellows' fish fry. That's how come I got swimming lessons pretty quick; *he'd* never learned how."

Brody saw to it that he kept in shape, doing push-ups morning and night, and eating sparely. With one exception, he never drank during the summer, going on the wagon resolutely the first of June, and descending from it with all flags flying on September twenty-first, the day after the beach club was officially closed.

He had never married. The first girl he was engaged to died of influenza during the epidemic in 1918, and the second one eloped with his best friend two days before the wedding. That was enough for him, and perhaps it was as well.

He was used to his life and did not think it bad, not really bad. In winters he drove a taxi in Pittsburgh, and had for twenty years. He owned his cab, was his own master, and worked hard during the week. Friday night and all day Saturday he devoted to the bottle, seldom (though sometimes) getting into fights or other involvements. Sunday he devoted to recovery, and on Monday he was at work again.

"I know I got a drinking problem," he said to one of his few friends. "But I don't let it lick me, I lick *it*. I don't give it its head but the two days each week, and not at all but the once in summertime."

The summer rift in his abstention took place always at the time of the equinoctial storm, whenever in September it might happen. On that day, when the "No swimming" sign was posted, Brody brought a bottle to the bathhouse, polished off a good part of it in his cubicle, and then went out to fight the sea.

"All right, you hoor!" he'd yell at the Atlantic. "Come on, now, none of your sass! I'm going to kill you, that's all. I'm going to chew you up and spit you out, that's all!"

The seas were sometimes frightful on those days, brawling, chaotic, with great ranges of marching water, and a boil of strong-smelling foam. Brody felt a murderous joy when he met the first wave and dived under it to come up the other side and meet the next one, cursing and belittling it, as the rain drove sideways and the spume lashed.

The children had been the first to discover this odd custom of his, and then their parents had found out about it, but since it was his one dereliction, if dereliction it could be called, they let it pass without rebuke. Actually they looked forward to it, and on that day, when attics were leaking and elm trees scraping, they could be seen, waterproofed groups on the bathhouse porch, watching Brody's private battle with the sea.

It made them feel good in a strange way, perhaps because they saw it as a demonstration of the fact that tyranny can sometimes be outwitted, rendered impotent, by a simple combination of skill and scorn; and each one thought of tyranny as a different thing.

"At least, thank God, he's never tackled a hurricane," said one, watching him.

"He'd probably lick it if he did," said another. "It's funny; he's nothing but a flea in all that water but he doesn't seem *reduced,* does he? Anyone else would but he doesn't."

They had learned, though, not to talk to him about it afterward. Not that he was ever stiff or resentful, but they could tell by a certain vagueness, perhaps sheepishness, in his response, that he would prefer to have the thing forgotten.

The summer of 1955, Brody's thirty-seventh at Clam Strand, was an unusually hot one. All during July the sun blazed in the sky, and the sea unfolded on the sand like rolls of silk. The children spent more of their day in the water than out of it, and even the oldest ladies came out of their cocoons and trembled into the sea, smiling, charmed by a sense of the revival of youth. Brody watched over them all, but no one needed saving, for the waves were gentle. His big body was brown all over and blotched and blotted with freckles of different magnitudes; in his darkened face his eyes had the pale color of chicory flowers.

One Saturday morning toward the end of the month he became aware that something was taking place. The people in their bathing suits were gathering together in a group, talking in low voices; several of them looked at him over their shoulders and quickly looked away again. Brody felt a vague presentiment that did not please him though he could not understand it; and then he saw that all of them, the children, the men and women, the stout ladies staggering up from umbrella shade, all were coming toward him, smiling. In the lead were Dr. Ruffin and Mr. Arnold Wheater, this

year's club president. The two men were carrying a large box
between them.

Brody got to his feet as if to face a posse.

It turned out that they were making him a present of a
small television set, because, as Dr. Ruffin said, in his courteous Southern voice, "Except for you, Brody, a lot of us
wouldn't even be here now. This is just an entirely inade-
quate"—he searched for some word other than "token," but
wound up with it anyhow—"*token* of what we feel toward
you. Of the deep, heartfelt gratitude and appreciation, and,
uh, *affection* that we feel toward you."

They waited expectantly for his delight, and he did not
disappoint them. "Why, I don't know what to say, sir, folks.
This is going to be a real companion for me evenings, a
wonderful companion. Better than a wife, even, they tell me,"
he said grinning, "because you can shut it off when you want
to. No, seriously," he said, making his face serious, "I just
don't know how to thank you all, you just don't know what
it means to me—"

It was also true that he did not know what it meant to
him. It seemed to bring an uneasiness with it, some feeling
of threat or sadness, and this was not because he already had
a set in Pittsburgh, and one with a twenty-one-inch screen.

The month of August, which began well, soon became un-
certain and disturbed. The first of the hurricanes, with its
foolish girl's name, cast its shadow far ahead. The sea lost its
rhyme and roared for days on one loud level, sounding from
a distance less like water than like fire. At night there seemed
to be another sound; a faint reverberation as of distant can-
nons or thunder, though the skies were clear. The summer
people battened down their hatches and the timid ones went
back to the city, but the storm missed them and went by, leaving only the same tormented seas and moody weather behind
it—one day fair, the next one cold or foggy.

On one of the fine days, Arnold Wheater dropped down on

the sand beside Brody, who was surprised; this did not often happen.

"Good morning, Brody."

"Good morning, sir."

"What do you think it's going to do?" Arnold said, nodding his head at the sky and meaning the weather.

"Hold fair awhile, anyway, I'd say."

"What about this new hurricane, Diane" (he gave it the French pronunciation). "Think we'll get her?"

"Well, it's a little too soon to tell, sir. We may, and then again we may not."

"I'd just as soon she got lost, myself. Mrs. Wheater and I put in twelve new trees last fall."

"Is that right, sir?" said Brody, nodding agreeably, as if this was news he had been waiting to hear. Arnold lighted a cigarette and held out the pack. "Care for one, Brody?"

"I don't smoke, sir. Only for a cigar now and then. Bad for the wind."

"You've got something there, all right. Wish I could quit myself. All this cancer talk, it gets so you sort of . . ." But he dropped the sentence, to which neither he nor Brody had been listening, and took a deep breath of smoke. "Brody?"

"Yes, sir?"

"Let me see, I was just wondering, you'll be sixty your next birthday, won't you?"

"Fifty-eight, sir," said Brody. So that's what it is, he thought.

"Oh. Fifty-eight, is it? Well, you got a lot of good years in you yet, Brody." He laughed. Brody thought the laugh meaningless and did not meet it. "That's why we think the time's just about come—a few of us were talking it over—the committee, that is—and we decided that it's—that after this September, you *deserve* to start taking things easy. I mean we have no right to go on taking up your time and your—your energies *forever*—"

"You mean you're firing me?" said Brody.

"Oh, for God's sakes, what a word!" Sweat broke out on Arnold's brow and nose. "Why, Brody, we'd never *fire* you.

It's just we think that the time's come for you to, for you to—"

"Retire," said Brody.

"Well, yes, that's more or less the word."

But Brody could not let any of his people feel uncomfortable, even Mr. Wheater, little "Arnie" Wheater, as he had been called, whom Brody had pulled out of a sea-puss by the seat of his scared pants, years ago, and whom he'd bawled hell out of for peeking through a knothole at Mrs. Palegrave taking off her clothes.

"I think maybe you're right, sir," he said. "I'd given it some thought myself. The job's for someone younger than I, now."

Relief almost brought tears to Arnold's eyes. He seized the lifeguard's hand in both his own, pressing it hysterically. "Gee, you're great, Brody, you're a great scout! You'll come to see us here and swim often, won't you? Promise?"

"Why sure, you bet," Brody said.

On the morning of Diane, Brody parked the Chevy in the beach-club parking space, which was now a shallow lake with waves running. How he had managed to reach there was a mystery to him; just getting out of the car took planning and effort, and after that he had to lean there a minute getting his bearings. Then he aimed himself at the bathhouse and started through the water, gripping his bottle close; not his first bottle, but his new, valuable one. On second thought he returned to the Chevy, opened the door, which all but blew out of his hand, took a good burning swig, and laid the bottle carefully on the back seat where it would be safer.

"You stay there and wait for me, now," he said to it.

Then he aimed himself at the bathhouse again and made his way, like a man making a rude sketch of something, to the steps. The walls of the roofless corridor knocked him back and forth between them, but he got free of them at last and burst out onto the veranda, where foam was washing over the boards.

He felt a pang of doubt as he held the railing to steady himself. His drunkenness had lifted for a moment, the way

it did sometimes when he was very drunk, and he saw everything pinned on the instant, sharp and clear. A bird was torn
across the sky, and he noticed how the railing and the whole
shallow building were shuddering in the blows of the wind.
All the empty cubicles were calling in different keys—he could
hear them even above the sea—and there was a powerful smell
of fish and depths.

But the doubt lasted only a moment. He took off his raincoat, which instantly blew away on a high northerly course.
He was glad to see that he had put on his swimming trunks,
though there was not a soul to watch him, this day. He took
the steps blindly, expecting shallow water on the sand, but
found instead that he was waist deep in the tide.

"All right, you hoor, goddamn you!" howled Brody, pushing
forward. "I'll kill you, that's all, I'll murder you! To hell with
you! To hell with you forever! You think I was ever scared
of you one minute of my life?"

Through the spume and rain he saw a great white wall
advancing on him and dived under it just in time. When he
came up again he was well beyond his depth and faced with
another marching wall, and when he got through that one he
saw there was another. They were running close and he was
conscious that his breath was getting short, but he churned on,
and between dives yelled at the water and the world and all
his life. The clouds ran low in herds above him; the rain
was so dense that it was almost as impossible to breathe with
his head above the surface as below it. Soon he was gasping
and in pain, and decided to turn back. Thunder ran with
the clouds, too, and sprigs of lightning hissed all around him
where they touched the water.

But lightning was not the brightest thing; hot sparks of
red and green and white snapped and dazzled in his eyeballs,
and his chest was so seared and taken up with pain that there
was no room for breathing. Everything was going very fast,
or was it too slow? When another water range bore down on
him he missed his dive, and when he came up from under
he could only whisper.

"Do it, then," he gasped, choking. "God damn you, get it done."

The last thing he saw, in a freakish parting of the rain, was the bathhouse sidling awkwardly along the beach like a great damaged crab, and he felt a faint detachment of surprise before the world went out.

A Name in Blue

Bonnadilla Benson never cared for the fact that she had been named for an apartment house. The time she resented it most, however, was the time when she resented everything most—when she was fifteen years old.

"They all call me Bonnie at school," she told her mother. "They always have. They think it's my real name and if they ever find out I'll die, that's all, I'll just die. How could you have done such a thing to me, named me a name like that, a little baby like I was!"

"Oh, it was that summer before you were born," said her mother with a certain soft remembering look that Bonnadilla simply could not stand. "It was the first time, it was the *only* time, that we ever lived in New York City. I've told you. That hot, hot summer. I used to go blocks out of my way just so I could walk through that one street to the grocery store. I went through it on purpose because there was a row of houses set back there with real little gardens out front, flowers with soot on them, and old raggedy bashed-in looking cats asleep under bushes—but gardens, anyway. I used to walk slowly, take my time. I was big as a house."

"Oh, *Mother!*" said Bonnadilla.

"I didn't care. I guess I never was so happy, before or since. I was so happy I felt as if I was dreaming all the time. I loved that city, noise and all, dirt and all."

"I wish you'd had me there and stayed there. This old dump. Mason City's all I ever get to."

"They still had some horses then; and sometimes there'd be one, a milk one, drawn up by the curb with a feed bag on his nose that he'd blow into, and the oats would puff out and sprinkle on the street, and down would come the sparrows out of nowhere, scrapping and yapping in and out around his hoofs as if they were—I don't know—rocks or cliffs or something safe like that. And then in the gardens, toward September, if I got out early enough, I'd see the morning-glories before they had a chance to get sooty; perfectly clean, like Harding morning-glories. Dewy, too. I never thought they'd have dew in a city—"

"But the apartment house, I mean."

"Well, it was there, next to these gardens. Just one of those old-style apartment houses trimmed with fire escapes, maybe eight, ten stories high. Bonnadilla Apartments. That's what it said on the front in gravestone letters, and on the doormat, and on the side of the building in big blue paint. Maybe they even had it printed on the roof for the planes to marvel at. I don't suppose it amounted to much, but I thought it looked just grand. There was a doorman, you know, and a tiled lobby and a switchboard; and the name—I thought it was a lovely name—was all mixed up with that last wonderful summer. So when you were born, a month after your daddy died—he died just a month before you were born—"

"Oh, Mother, I *know* that," cried Bonnadilla with the furious adolescent impatience which is nourished by the words of parents. "You've told me that about sixty million times already."

"*I* don't know where you get your disposition. . . . Anyhow, I just thought of that name for you and it seemed to mean a lot to me at the time. I still think it's pretty."

"I don't. It's bad enough to be named for some old dead relation, but gosh, being named for some dumb old *apartment* house."

"Well, goodness, there was a boy back home in Harding

whose parents had named him for a Pullman car. I think that's much worse. Royal G. Schermer, he was."

"It sounds like a real name, though, not like a horse or a disease or something."

"G was for Gorge. Royal Gorge. I think that's terrible. Royal Gorge Schermer."

Bonnadilla could not bring herself to agree out loud with her mother, but she did say, "My. What was the matter with *his* folks to call him that?"

"I believe it was the name of the Pullman car they took on their wedding trip."

"Oh, *Mother!*" said Bonnadilla.

She never saw New York City until she was forty, when her husband was transferred, rather late in life, to the Eastern branch of his company. Harry and she (she had been Bonnie Herrick for many years then) had had their children young; all three were nicely out of the way, in college.

The first month or two had been spent finding a place to live in and then settling it; trying to learn east from west and north from south. When Bonnie rode on the subway she was always coming up from under some river in the wrong place; and for a long time the noise bothered her, the daytime clatter and the nighttime grumble, but after a while custom began to set in and then she found a wonderful new way to enjoy herself. She had not yet begun her city friendships, the apartment was all finished and smelled stingingly of fresh paint and fresh fabric; for the first time since her marriage there was nothing that she needed to do. It was April, and warm for once. In the mornings when Harry had gone she would leave the house and start walking, never caring what her destination was to be. Along the avenues, along the streets, she walked, looking at all the faces among which there was so seldom a Face, staring into the shopwindows, entering the great swarming stores, riding the escalators, touching the jewels. She found the scurvied groves of the public parks, and the Egyptian rooms at the museum where the faces of antiquity looked out at her with a strange sibling calm.

In her wandering she experienced a state of tranced contentment that she could not remember having felt since her youth. She tried to describe it to Harry, but he, though he loved her, had long since become afflicted with a sort of domestic deafness; she could see his eyes glaze and his fingers twitch at the edges of the evening paper as she talked.

"Honestly, Harry," said Bonnie, "catching your interest is like trying to catch a wild coati-mundi. I give up. I swear I do give up."

"Why, listen, I heard every word you said. You said that when you're out walking and staring that way you forget you are a person at all. You said you feel as if you are just a pair of eyes, walking—"

"Oh, I know you heard what I said, but you didn't *listen.* Never mind. I hear but I don't listen when you talk about consumer interest and the fiscal year."

One day, late in the month, she found herself in a downtown section of the city. The day was fine, with a filmy light, and on one corner a man stood beside a rackety little cart trimmed with flags and filled with tulips. Every now and then he cawed a word or two. Beyond him, to the left, there were trees, and Bonnie came upon a row of galleried old-fashioned houses set far back from the street with door yards in front of them. There the privet bushes were stiffly beaded with green, and out of the earth amongst gum papers, little gaggles of sedum leaves were showing, and crocuses, shaped like egg-cups, stood open to the sun. Crocuses! Flowers! Bonnie stopped walking suddenly and looked up at the cliffside of the apartment house which rose beyond the little gardens. There in huge faded printing she saw her name, BONNADILLA, as if the Lord had spoken.

Slowly she put out her hand and took hold of a picket. So there had really been a time, a time past imagining, when she, unborn, had traveled through this street. One never quite believes in the myth of other people's lives before one's own began, but now this name in flaking blue, this aging building, the tattered gardens, all her seniors, forced upon her the jarring consideration that once her mother had been a person in her own right; an ego with feelings, not just Mother (oh, you know *Mother*) but a human being with thoughts and wishes she could never guess.

There was a chatter and turmoil; three sparrows fell out of an ailanthus tree in a scuffle. Involuntarily she turned her head to see a horse and wagon at the curb, but there was nothing but a parked truck: Pfanzer Bros. Dry Cleaning While U Wait.

Half reluctantly she began to walk toward the apartment building. On the backs of her hands there were already age freckles, and she could feel the deep wrinkle between her eyebrows as if a finger had been laid there. Life was nothing but a minute, after all.

Above the doorway of the building the name, as her mother had told her, stood out in gravestone letters, but the doormat was gone. She stood there, peering into the dimness of the hall. A breath of old discouraged air breathed out at her; a mortal breath, and she felt very mortal.

"Yes, ma'am?"

She had not noticed the man leaning against one of the machine-made pillars; faded drinkworn face, soiled shirt, trousers that might have been part of a uniform.

"I was wondering about the origin of the name of this building. It—it interests me."

"Why it's named the *name* it is?"

"Yes. Is there anyone who might know?"

He scratched his head with the tip of his smallest finger; a gesture implying at the same time refinement and serious thought.

"Miss Pavane might, I guess. Her father was the one that built it. Likely he named it."

"Can I—does she live here?"

"Yeah. She lives here." He looked at her appraisingly, and Bonnie willed an air of respectability upon herself.

"I'll show you to her apartment," he decided, and she followed him across the dim lobby, where some of the tiles had been chipped away, to the door of a ground-floor apartment.

The woman who presently opened the door was short, fat, and elderly, with flame-colored hair and a flowered dress. When Bonnie explained why she had come, the woman said, "But how does it happen that you want to know?"

"It's my name, too. Bonnadilla," Bonnie admitted for the first time since her childhood.

"Why, is it? Why, how interesting. Why, how *interesting*. Come in, come in."

Miss Pavane waddled chintzily into her choked living room and offered Bonnie a chair and a cigarette. The room was a hive of patterns and objects: the wallpaper was patterned and covered with pictures, the rug was patterned and covered with smaller rugs, patterned. The couch and large crouching chairs were riotous with patterns of vegetation. In the windows, aspidistra plants, fierce as moray eels, struck upward from pots of varicosed majolica, and they were still trimmed with the red Christmas ribbons of years ago. This was the sort of place where the carnival kewpie wound up its days, along with the signed photograph of General Pershing, the laughing Buddha, and the plaster-of-paris cupids' heads mounted on a velvet plaque.

"Now, how in the world, in the *world*, did you happen to have that name?" said Miss Pavane, blowing out smoke.

"My mother saw it on this building. Long ago. She liked it."

"Now, did you ever! Well, it's a lucky name. My father got it off a Pullman car."

"Oh, no!" said Bonnie.

"Why, yes, why not?"

"Just—it surprised me."

"My father was a farmer back in Oklahoma, see. And poor. Poor as Job's turkey. The land was no good, but how he worked, oh, nobody works like that these days. Well, we were so poor we didn't have anything. Anything. Bare boards and washtubs, that's everything I remember about our house. Not one toy. Not one picture, only the calendar the feed store put out and we stopped getting that when our credit ran dry. Well, when I get big I'm going to have *things,* I said. . . ." Miss Pavane's eyes, glossy as beetles, traveled over her storehouse of comforts and atrocities.

"And then, did you ever, one day when he was forty-six years old and worn raw, just raw, from work, and so was my mother, what did they do but find there was oil on the place. Oil. And overnight, almost, we had more money than we knew what to do with. My father said, 'What's the most different place there is on earth from here?' And then he said, 'New York City,' and then he said, 'And that's where we're going to go and we're going to stay at.' So we packed up our new clothes and put them in our new grips and he bought us all, all seven of us, Pullman tickets on the train going East. We'd never seen anything like it in our lives. The white tidies on the backs of the chairs, the porter with his whisk broom (colored, and we'd never seen a colored person before) and the dining car with a rose and a fern on every table. Well, it was the other side of the world to us, just the other side of the world. And the name of *our* car—"

"Was the Bonnadilla!" cried Bonnie.

"Was the Bonnadilla *Flats,*" corrected Miss Pavane.

"Flats" is the last straw, thought Bonnie, but she said nothing.

"And so because it was the first real differentness from our old life, the first new *place,* I mean, the name of that car was like a—what do you call it—like a *symbol* to my father. After he'd been here a while he bought this piece of real estate and built this building. He wanted to call it just like it was on the car—Bonnadilla Flats—but my mother, who'd been doing some noticing, said, no, apartments sounded better, and that's how it all was."

Bonnie stood up and thanked her, but Miss Pavane seemed reluctant to have her go.

"And it's been like a symbol to me, too," she said. "It's been more than a symbol; it's been my home and my bread and butter and my family. Because when my father died, and the money was just about gone, he left me this building. All to me, because I was the only one of us that never married."

"Harry," said Bonnie that evening, "how do they name Pullman cars?"

"Hmm?" said Harry. "How do they what?"

"Name Pullman cars. How do they pick out the names for them?"

"Well, for God's sake. Why?"

"I just was wondering."

"I think they name them for places mainly. Probably places along the route, something like that. But why, for God's sake?"

"I was just wondering."

The next day she bought herself a world atlas, and there, yes, in the index she found what she was looking for: Bonnadilla Flats, Gopher, Nev; pop: 59.

"Pop: fifty-nine," said Bonnie. "Why, it's hardly a town at all," and when she closed the atlas, she thought that she had done with it for good.

But the idea of Bonnadilla Flats would not be done for. It lay just under her thoughts, humming persistently, like a seashell to the ear. She considered it fate and nothing else when her dearest friend, in California, invited her to her daughter's wedding. Accepting with alacrity, Bonnie left a day or two beforehand, as stimulated and secretive as a woman on her way to sin. Harry took her to the airport, looking rather puzzled; she had never wanted to fly before.

"Why now?" he asked.

"It's time I had the experience," she said firmly.

Soon she found herself in the air, seated for many hours among traveling salesmen and lonely widows. For the first time she was able to look down with the eye of patronage on wrinkled mountain ranges, cities, counties, prairies marked with rivers plain as gravy-trees on a carving board, and at last she came to earth on a tilted sun-baked land with her ears cracking and her eyes dazzled.

"Bonnadilla Flats?" said the man at the bus station. "Don't nobody much go out there any more, but I guess Verne can run a little ways off his route."

"I'm doing some research on that town," said Bonnie. "Is there anyone there who might help me? Tell me how it got its name, for instance?"

"Old Eli Carson could if anyone could. He's lived there all his life; right up against ninety years. He runs the post office and store. Did, anyways."

"Bonnadilla Flats?" said the bus driver later. "First time I've had a call for there in I don't know when. Go six miles out of the way to get you there at all. Dead," he said. looking at her curiously. "There ain't nothing deader than a shrunk-up town."

Still dazed and ringing from the heights and distances of her journey, Bonnie sat staring out of the window. Great wastes of sage were speeding by, miles of silver tufts like a forest of tiny olive trees. The air was strong with their dry smell. Gophers stood praying at their doorways, and the sky was pale with heat. Far away, but drawing nearer, the mountains rose in blue, like an arrested sea. How old the earth is, Bonnie thought. Here it is, just as it was; no beauticians, no despoilers, have had a hand in this. Here's the truth, the whole truth and nothing but the truth, so help me God.

What was left of Bonnadilla Flats stood on the level desert floor, but close beyond it were the foothills of mountains, no longer blue. When one was near them they were brown as army blankets, shabby and patched, and the wooden town was silvery from weather, like the sage.

She got down from the bus feeling stiff and disconcerted. What had she expected to see? "Back at two," the driver said. "And we don't wait."

The stillness was shocking. In the blinding road lizards

stood transfixed and panting; a beer can blazed in the sun.
The air seemed stretched thin with heat, as if in a moment a
sound would come from it, a resonance high and quivering.

Most of the houses were abandoned shells, but children's
toys lay in the yards of some, and there was a smell of food.
The feeling of regard, of being watched, came from the close,
overbearing hills. A chicken in a gateway stood on one large
claw and made a querulous, noonday sound.

At the center of the street stood the Bonnadilla Flats Post
Office and General Store; Elisha Carson, Prop. The letters on
the dusty glass were old fashioned, with thorns on them. A
veil of flies danced winningly around Bonnie's head, and she
opened the screen door quickly and stepped inside.

It was dark in there after the street, and it smelled of times
past and the memories of merchandise. The old man, Elisha
Carson, sat in the cave of his store; as she came in he got
slowly to his feet. In the shadows he had a sort of luster of
age; his taut skin and polished scalp, the knuckles of his
hands, all had a faint gleam to them, and his shirt was white,
and his old eyeglasses had golden rims.

"Yes, ma'am, what can I do for you?" His manner was
courteous, and, like the letters on his store window, old
fashioned.

"I thought that you might have the answer to my riddle.
My first name, you see, is Bonnadilla. My mother took the
name from an apartment house in New York City; the man
who built the apartment house got the name from a Pullman
car; the Pullman people named it for this town—"

"And this town was named for— Why, yes, sit down. I'll
tell you all about the name. It started here; you've found the
source, ma'am."

The old man sat down slowly, attentive to his joints, and
Bonnie sat too, beside his ancient rolltop desk. The string
dispenser hung like a top in the air, and flies, indoors as well
as out, buzzed on a desultory musing note.

Elisha Carson was silent for a moment as though gathering
up strength, along with recollection, for the recital he was to

give. Many times, while he was speaking, he paused to clear the age away from his voice, or to listen for a memory.

"Now, as I recall, ma'am, from what I've heard, the first settler, Percival Fortinbrass, came out here about eighteen hundred and fifty, or fifty-one. He came prospecting; just up and left his farm back in Connecticut to come out here and try his luck. And he found it. He struck silver ore just about first thing, staked out his claim, built him a house, and then the others came. Soon it was a town, and prosperous at the time. (You'd never guess it now, though, would you?) Now, this Mr. Fortinbrass had nobody for his family but one little girl, three or four years of age, I would say. The reason he had come West was that he'd lost his wife and three prior children from the typhoid fever, and he set all the store in the world by this one little girl. Her name was Bonnadilla. Bonnadilla Fortinbrass. Her mother had made up the name herself. She was a woman claimed she wanted each of her children to have a name that nobody else had. I don't recollect what all the other names had been, but one, I know, a boy, had been called Colossus Rhodes.

"Now, of course, this little girl was who he named the town for. He was the first settler so he got to name it. Bonnadilla Flats. She was a good deal older than I was and I never exactly knew her, but she was the kind who leaves a lot of talk behind her, and leaves it for a long time. Her father, Mr. Fortinbrass, never married again—just seemed to concentrate his interests on this one child—and she grew up spoiled and wild. Maybe she would have been, no matter what, because she was different from other folks, or at least the ones in these parts. One thing that made her different—she was beautiful, but that's not much; most young folks are beautiful, as you can see when you get to my time of life—but she had this hair. It was the color—let me see—it was *blonde*, of course, but it was the color of— Well, when I was a boy we used to have taffy pulls. Molasses taffy was the kind we made and when you had worked the material and worked it and twisted it, it got to be this very pale color, kind of silvery. That was the color her hair was, but the other thing about it was that it was so long that it reached clear down to her ankles. Silvery-gold, and long as a cape. Oh, I saw her! I wasn't any more than knee-high to a duck, but I remember her! Riding her horse like an Indian, or just switching along on her own two feet, with this hair hanging down her back, and every boy in town after her, and every man, married or not, helping himself just to the sight of her.

"Oh, but she was wild and bold, ma'am! She was bad. Reckless. Her father, Mr. Fortinbrass, got so concerned about her after a while that he married her off to a Mormon gentleman fifty-five years of age. He already had three wives, settled ladies, all of them, and twenty-two children, most of them older than this Bonnadilla was herself. He was very well thought of in Salt Lake City. My father told me he was very well thought of, and so was all his family up to then. But when this young lady, Bonnadilla, came into the household there was trouble. She set two of these prior wives against each other to the point where one of them—Jemima? Keziah? She was named for one of the daughters born to Job after his trials, I recall—well, *she* took after the other with a hot flat-iron! Fortunately they stopped her in time, but think of it, ma'am; these two settled ladies!

"The next thing was a quarrel over her between two of the Mormon gentleman's grown sons. *Her* sons, too, in the eyes of the Mormon church, I presume. Oh, that was a serious fight; one boy shot the other in the hip. The boy didn't die, but it killed the Mormon gentleman; he came down with a stroke and was dead in a day. Did she stay and mourn? Did she grieve? No, sir, not she. What *she* did was to light out with a wealthy consumptive come West for his health. It didn't take her long to finish him off, and then she was richer by something in the neighborhood of fifty thousand dollars."

"Good gracious!" said Bonnie.

"Yes, you are named for a Jezebel, ma'am, a real Jezebel," said Mr. Carson. "I am sorry to have to tell you."

"Oh, that's perfectly all right," said Bonnie, feeling won-

derfully well and exhilarated; then she modified her tone. "I
mean since it's nobody I know or am related to, and since it
happened so long ago . . ."

"Ah, but you haven't heard the worst of it, ma'am. The
next thing anyone heard was that she had gone to Paris,
France, and was married to a count or a baron or some one
of those French titles they have over there. (Her third marriage, and she wasn't twenty-five!) Well, she had *jewels*, she
had a kind of a castle or a palace to live in, and carriages and
teams, and pet dogs, and I don't know what. That all came
out later in the newspapers. Even over here it was in all the
papers because it was such a scandal and, of course, because
she came from here. I can remember it myself, though I was
just a boy at the time. I remember the photo of her that they
printed: all that hair was braided and coiled around and
around her head like a kind of tower. Her face looked real
little underneath it, with these great big eyes she had and
the dimple that was in her chin. Oh, yes, she was handsome,
all right."

Mr. Carson paused. He gazed at his knuckles, raised his
chin, and gazed at the string dispenser. He cleared his throat
again before speaking. "Now, it seems that Bonnadilla, after a
while, was not exactly—well, ma'am, she was not exactly *true*
to her husband, this count or this baron or whatever he was.
And he found out about it, and do you know what he did?
Oh, he was of a very jealous disposition, and impulsive. Do
you know how he punished her? The servant girl peeked in
and saw it happen (being rich they had a lot of this French
help). Well, sir, when she took her hair down one night (she
wore it in a great big braid around her head, remember), he
waited till it was hanging down her back, this big braid, and
then, quick as lightning, he grabbed a razor and cut it off!
Right off close to her head. 'This hairdo should keep you
home for awhile,' he says, or some such thing, in French
of course. *She*, Bonnadilla, gave one scream, the servant girl
said, and then after that she didn't say a word; didn't cry,
didn't carry on, was perfectly quiet. She just leaned over and

picked up that braid and held it. *He* went into his room and
drank himself senseless. But the next morning"—Mr. Carson
leaned forward, gleaming frostily—"the next morning they
found him, this count or baron, dead in his bed. Strangled.
And you know what he had been strangled with? Yes, sir,
ma'am, that is correct. With Bonnadilla's braid of hair!"

The old man leaned back in his chair, as if the recital
had exhausted him pleasantly.

"But what happened to *her*, then?" cried Bonnie.

Mr. Carson spread his fingers. "Who knows? She disappeared. They never found her, or if somebody did find her it
never came to light. She had her ways with men, even crop-
headed, I'll be bound. Who knows? Why, she may be alive
today. But, no," he said regretfully, as Bonnie rose. "No,
probably not. She would have to be one hundred years of
age at least. No, probably not," he said.

When Harry met her at the airport a few days later, he
looked at her with pleased surprise. "Why, you look wonderful, Bonn. Bright and rested. So much better than you've *been*
looking."

"That's not just the way a woman likes to have a compliment phrased, darling, but thanks anyway."

In the cab she took his hand.

"You know, Harry, I have a confession to make to you.
Almost no one knows what I'm about to tell you; even Dr.
Ogle didn't know it when he married us. I don't know why
Mother let me get away with that unless she felt remorseful.
You know how you've always thought my name was just plain
Bonnie? Well, listen—no, now really *listen*, Harry, because
this is interesting . . ."

At
Seven
Cedars

On the island, when I was a child, our next-door neighbor was Miss Bella Barrington, a lady who washed hair. She did not wave it, set it, cut it, or dye it, she simply washed it. Tucked in the right front window of her house was a card that bore the one word SHAMPOOS; and over the little visor above the front door there was another sign, a shingle, on which the name of her house, Seven Cedars, was burned into the wood in imitation handwriting. This name must have had a particular meaning or value for her, because I have heard that when her father died and she inherited the house she at once went out and bought seven medium-sized cedar trees and had them planted in the back yard; then she ordered the sign. Perhaps she had been wanting to do this for years. Three of the cedars died quite soon but she never had them removed; they stood beside the others, stiff, auburn-colored trees that crackled brusquely when the east wind blew.

On the fine summer days one could almost always see one or two ladies in that yard, sitting in little rocking chairs drying their hair in the sun. They would each have a towel over the shoulders, and over that, in a capelet, lay their hair (many women had long hair in those days). From time to time they would raise their hands and flap their locks or run a comb through them, never reminding anybody of the Lorelei. When she considered that the ladies were fairly well "done" Miss

Barrington would come tripping from her house, hairbrush in hand.

She was the only woman I have ever seen to whom the verb "tripping," in the sense of a dainty walk, could be applied. It suited her exactly. The era of the Gibson girl and the straight-front shirtwaist was a thing of the remote past even then, but it must also have been the era of Miss Barrington's happiest recollection, since she refused to leave the fashion behind. She even retained the curious walk, canted forward from the waist as though led by her bosom, which was commanding, and she was latched into a most rigorous corset which aided the effect; it jutted out, visibly, in two little gables at her shoulder blades, and again in two little gables at the back of her hips. I often saw this corset drying on the line, where it had the look of some strange battledress with its many bones, buckles, garters, clasps, hooks, and laces, and wearing it would, I thought, be like wearing a close scaffolding. The large things about Miss Barrington were her bust and her head, which was wreathed about with a great, grand wealth of red-gold hair, natural, and an untold asset to her business. The small things about her were her feet; they were tiny, and she wore little kid button boots with high heels, and it was on these that she "tripped."

In her yard, beside the four live cedars and the three dead ones, there was a red pine that must have been very old, and whose boughs could easily be reached by first climbing the fence at the back of our garden. Often when there was nothing better to do I would get up into the tree and sit there looking out at the boats in the harbor and listening to the conversation of Miss Barrington and the lady whose hair she was brushing. It was often dull.

"It's been coming out a lot," the lady might say. "It's thinner, isn't it, Miss Barrington? Don't you think it's getting terribly thin?"

"Well, dear," Miss Barrington would say, brush, brush. "It's coming out a *little;* do you think maybe it could be the

Change?" Brush, brush. "Ladies often lose hair during the Change, you know."

Change? What Change? I wondered. Miss Barrington made the word sound charged, mysterious, the way it sounded in the poem "Full Fathom Five," but as far as I could see there was nothing rich or strange about the middle-aged lady down below.

I heard a lot about hair, and all the ills that hair is heir to: it was always falling out or losing its curl or breaking off or turning gray, and was the cause of great concern and conversation. Sometimes, though, and this was what I liked, hair was replaced as a subject by gossip.

"He always says she has a wild-rose color," Miss Barrington said, speaking of Dr. Loomis, the minister, and his wife. "But I happen to know—of course, this is in confidence—"

"Oh, of course!"

"Dear, it's *rouge* she uses. It's *rouge!* She has this little box of cake-rouge and she keeps it hidden in a pocket of her shoe bag. Oh, if he ever found out it would *kill* him!"

"I always thought she had a feverish appearance," the lady said. "I was worried it was her lungs."

"Rouge, dear. Roger and Gallet rouge is all that afflicts *her* lungs." The two ladies enjoyed a hearty laugh, and I tittered in the tree.

Sometimes I was myself the victim of Miss Barrington's brush. About twice a summer my mother's eye would fall with displeasure on my long lank curls. "It looks like kelp, Sally," she might say. "Why on earth won't you wear a bathing cap? I declare it *smells* like kelp. I'm going to make an appointment with Miss Barrington."

At this I would howl in protest, knowing as I did so that the howl was useless and that that day or the next would find me dropping the knocker on Miss Barrington's front door, which was always firmly closed. Dr. Melrose Barrington was the name engraved on the brass doorplate, for her father had been an army surgeon before his retirement.

"Good morning, dear, come in," Miss Barrington would say,

opening the door and gesturing inward with the brush or
comb she was holding. (I don't think I ever saw her empty-
handed in my life.) Reluctantly I would enter the darkish
house and go into the living room where mirrors and two
hand basins had been installed. As Miss Barrington combed
the tangles out of my hair I stared at the pictures on her wall:
a Campbell Kid by Grace G. Drayton, disguised as Bo-Peep,
a sepia print of Andrea del Sarto's Madonna, a sepia print of
the Angelus, an embroidered statement under glass: "This
too, shall pass away," and, dominating all, a very large tinted
photograph of Miss Barrington's father, the late surgeon. In
his whole bald butchery face, which had been treated to a
wash of pink, only his black-caterpillar eyebrows resisted soft-
ening; under his wooden mustache the photographer had
given him a woman's mouth, rosy-red and sweetly scalloped.
The effect was horrible, even frightening, and I was not sorry
when it was time for me, holding a folded towel to my eyes,
to lean forward in an attitude of prayer and let my hair be
washed.

Afterward, seated in the rocker in the back yard, I felt released, purged, as though I had come through an ordeal, and
this was something of the case, for Miss Barrington always got
soapsuds in my eye, and when she brushed she pulled. Even
her conversation was a trial: she always, every time, asked me
how old I was, how I liked school, and who my little friends
were; but on occasion she could be interesting. She told me,
for instance, that Alice Velter had once caught "bugs" in her
hair and had had to have her head soaked in kerosene every
day for a week. Alice was rich, stuck-up, and a year older
than I, and of course I was glad to have this information.

Miss Barrington's little business grew and prospered to the
point where she found it necessary, in summertime, to employ
an assistant. The first two years she had a taciturn Finnish
woman, but the third summer she had a new one, a girl from
Boston, named Isola. This name was pronounced not, as one

would expect, like the Italian word meaning island, but with its own arbitrary accent: Eye-*Sola*, like that.

She was a slim, sallow, pretty young woman with unusually luminous dark eyes that looked always as if they were sparkling with tears. Her hair was dark and curly. I have since wondered if she had not, perhaps, some colored blood. Though she was young, I remember in her a quality that was pensive, depleted in some way. I liked her very much, and she liked me. In the mornings before her work began and in the evenings when it was over we would talk and play games together. She was wonderful at this, and even then I sensed it, for when most grown people played with children one could feel the tension underneath, the waiting for the play to end, and the pretense of pleasure. But Isola did not pretend; she enjoyed those games as if she were a child herself.

I remember one morning early in the summer, on first waking, I looked out of my window and saw Isola standing in the yard next door; she was in her neat white uniform, looking out towards the harbor, holding a sprig of honeysuckle to her nose.

I decided to surprise her and ran downstairs and out of doors in my pajamas. I stole across the cold grass, through the gap in the hedge, and up behind her. Then I seized her around the waist and shouted "Boo!"

Isola screamed and then laughed and turned to struggle with me. "Why, you little sneaky! Why, you little villain! Scaring me out of my skin like that! I'll show you, oh, I'll show *you!*" She began to tickle me, and I broke away and ran around the yard and she ran after me, and both of us were laughing.

"Well, what's going on?" said the milkman coming around to the back door. He was smiling at us, and I saw him see Isola for the first time and I knew he liked her. "And who is this young lady?"

"She's Miss Barrington's new hairwasher," I said. "Her name's Isola. What's your last name, Isola?"

"Deacon," she said, and she was smiling at him, too, over

my head, and after he left she asked me questions about him.

Our milkman, a widower, was named Mr. Beausire. Peg was the name of his horse. I knew them both well. Sometimes he had taken me along on his milk route, and those are mornings I shall never forget. Nobody had used the day yet, and nobody had used me much, either, nor I my life. Everything was new. The sun would still be low and the air quiet. Dew sent out great rays from grasses, and swallows were beaded along the wires. People's dogs, just let out, would be trotting briskly, singly or in pairs, across the fields and roads, as if to urgent appointments. "Business dogs," Mr. Beausire called them.

Peg ambled her polished hindquarters along as we went from house to house.

"Hold the reins please, Sally," Mr. Beausire would say and drop the old smoothed leather straps into my hands as if Peg really needed controlling. She paid no attention. She switched her tail, shivered her skin, and leaned her long head down in the clover where her chewing sounded like people walking through swamps.

Clinkety clink, back would come Mr. Beausire with his basket of empties. "Didn't try to bolt with you, did she, Sally? Ah, she's a fire-breather, she's a mustang! Giddy-ap, Peg."

The last house of all was washed up in a meadow. There in the chicory and toadflax by the road so many small white butterflies were moving that they seemed to shimmer like spangles.

Peg knew where she was headed on the return journey. The bottles chimed in their containers as she trotted briskly, and her mane and tail blew sideways, long and graceful. When I got home I was ravenous, and the smell of bacon came out of our house almost calling my name. . . .

But the point of it all is that Mr. Beausire was a widower. Not old, not young; in his forties, probably. He was a well-set-up man with nice blue eyes and a thick mustache that died at the corners. When he laughed—I remember it now but I didn't know I was noticing it then—he had two long cracks of dimples in his cheeks. Also he owned his own dairy, had no dependents, and was eligible in every way.

The sound of Peg's hoofs, the scrape of the wagon wheel, were usually the first sounds I heard on waking. Then clinkety clink, clinkety clink, along our side yard to the back porch steps. Next, it was Miss Barrington's turn and very often I would hear her voice greeting him in an ironical arch way.

"Good morning, sir!"

"Morning, Miss Barrington. You're up with the birds as usual."

"Oh, I think morning's the best part of the day, don't you?"

Then she would always invite him to come in and have a cup of coffee before going on his "weary way." Sometimes he accepted the offer and sometimes he didn't. It was no secret in our house that Miss Barrington had her eye on him. "Ah, he's got no time for her," said Bridie, our cook. "She's old enough to be his mother!" I knew this was not true, but had learned that people always used these words if a woman was *any* older than a man.

Sometimes that summer it happened that Isola would be the one to greet Mr. Beausire; and then for a long time I could hear the murmur of their voices before Peg started up again or Miss Barrington interrupted them: "Mr. Beausire, I wonder if you know it's nearly seven. Isola, he's a *very busy* man. . . ."

One night in August my parents gave a large dinner party. I knew it was to be a special one because of the long groaning of the ice-cream freezer on the back porch, because of the champagne bottles in the icebox, and the fact that Bridie was going to make meringues.

I was banished to my room at seven with the understanding that I need not go to bed until dinner was over, when Bridie would send me up some of the party dessert. I waited patiently, listening to the bursts of greeting and then the gathering clack and babble; louder when they all went into the dining room, directly below. But it took them forever to eat their dinner, they were so slow with their talking and laughing. I grew tired of my room and slipped down the stairs to wait outdoors. It was a warm dark night. As I went by the dining room I could see the ladies in their blue and white and silver dresses; the men in their starched shirts and little bow ties. I was like the mermaid in Andersen's fairy tale gazing in at the lighted ship and I knew it was sad; not for me, but for them, enclosed as they were, old as they were, in their little lighted vessel of festivity.

I went down to the corner of our garden and felt my way up into the pine tree, and sat there peacefully, looking out at the clear harbor lights. It was still; I could hear men talking on one of the boats way off, and in the background the buzz and gabble of the grown-up party. But presently I heard another sound, and looking over my shoulder I saw that someone, someone darker than the darkness, was walking softly across Miss Barrington's yard. Not knowing that I was up in the branches, the person, a man, walked slowly to the pine tree and leaned against it; I heard him sigh. I was frightened, but I need not have been, because in a few minutes Isola came out of the house and ran silently across the grass, her white uniform glimmering, straight to the tree, straight to the man. He pulled her into his arms and I knew it was Mr. Beausire.

"Hello," I said.

I saw the dim whiteness of their upturned faces and then Isola laughed softly. "Why, look, we got a little owl above us. What you doing up there this time of night, little owl?"

"Waiting for my dessert," I said.

"What do they give you? Slugs? Field mice?" asked Mr. Beausire, in a low voice, and both of them laughed, still in very low voices.

"Peach ice cream and meringues and whipped cream on top!" I said, and hearing Millie, the maid, beginning to call my name, I scrambled down out of the tree, all needle-scratched and greedy.

What wakened me next morning was the sound of the milk

wagon, but so much earlier than usual that I got up to look out of the window. It was hardly light at all, but I was able to see Mr. Beausire standing on the curb, lifting Isola down from the wagon. He held her against him for a minute, close and still. She whispered something to him and he whispered something back, and then she gave a quick look at Miss Barrington's windows, put her finger to her lips and turned away, running noiselessly along the side yard to the back door.

I did not like what I had seen. It made me feel lonesome, left-out and queer, and when I went back to sleep I dreamed about it. But later, roughhousing in the sea with my friends, the matter was forgotten.

By five o'clock, waterlogged and at peace, I was sitting in the field beyond our garden making a basket out of cockleburs. The last of Miss Barrington's ladies had pinned up her hair and gone home, but I could hear voices in her house talking and talking, though I could not hear the words, and then there was a very strange loud sound; was it laughing? *Crying?* No, it had to be laughing; there were only grown-up ladies in that house. I watched the sailboats in the harbor all folding into place, finished with racing; the water below them was dyed deep with afternoon. . . . And then my peace was jarred by the sudden rude burst of a firecracker. I felt exasperated; I knew it was the work of Romley Reamer, a horrible boy several houses away, who always kept a few firecrackers after the Fourth to fray people's nerves with.

"That nut, Romley," I said disgustedly, throwing away the bur basket. "I detest that nut!" I got up and walked slowly and nonchalantly toward the house. I also detested firecrackers.

"Dear!" called Miss Barrington unexpectedly, coming out of her back door. "Dear, could you come here a minute?"

As I approached her I saw that her red-gold hair was hanging down her shoulder, that on her cheek were four thin stripes of red, and that in her hand she held a big old-fashioned pistol. I thought she was dressed up for a joke; some kind of grown-up joke.

She smiled at me in a queer way. "Listen, dear, I just killed Isola. You better go tell your mama."

I gaped at her.

"She stole the man I love, she *stole* him, and I killed her. Hurry up now, dear, go get your mother." She gestured with the pistol, not threateningly, but as she had so often gestured with the brush and comb, as if she were giving me a little push from a distance, and it was this movement, for some reason, that showed me she was saying a true thing. My heart split into several hearts, all bolting, and I ran screaming up the back porch steps. "*Maa*-ma! *Maa*-ma!"

"What in the world!" cried Bridie, in the kitchen. "Your Ma's out. Did something sting you, or what?"

"Her!" I gasped, pointing. "Her! She's killed Isola!"

Bridie started to laugh, but then she leaned to look out and saw Miss Barrington waiting, with the pistol in her hand and the scratch on her face and her hair all down.

"Jesus of Nazareth," she said, and pulled me close. "Millie, lock the door!"

But Millie, a weak greenish woman, had fainted on the kitchen floor. Bridie released me, stepped over Millie, hooked the door, stepped back over Millie, took me up where she had left off, and pulled me with her to the pantry phone.

"Hush your noise now, Sally. Stop it! I'm calling the police."

So Miss Barrington vanished from the island, and almost, after a while, from my thoughts. A family named Goucher bought the house next door and chopped down the dead cedars; they had four children and a dog, so the place was too noisy to be haunted.

But two years later when my Aunt Dora arrived to spend the summer she had news for my mother. "Opal, you'll die when I tell you. Listen. On the way down to the boat, our train stopped for no reason that I could see—another train coming, or something like that—and it stopped right beside the iron palings of that big lunatic asylum, you know? The State one? And what do you think I saw? Who do you think I saw? *Well, there,* sitting in rocking chairs on the asylum grass were three—I suppose *inmates,* with their hair spread out on their shoulders, drying in the sun, and who should be flitting to and fro among them, with a hairbrush, but—"

"But Miss Barrington!" cried my mother.

"Miss Barrington," agreed my aunt. "Honestly, Opal, what struck me was that those women didn't look one bit crazier than you or I or any other woman drying her hair outdoors. And then just as the train started Miss Barrington looked up and saw me! Our eyes met, and I bowed very slowly and seriously like Queen Mary from her Daimler or something, and she bowed back."

My mother stared at my aunt, then both of them burst into helpless laughter. I watched them. Was it funny? In a minute I laughed, too.

Another
Tune
for
Hecate

But that was when I was a *young* man," August said. His deep, pleasing voice was still faintly tinted with an accent. "A very, very young man; the age when one is proud like a rooster and foolish and loud like a rooster. And why not, after all? It is the one time in life when a man can shout about daybreak." He laughed pleasantly; his teeth were as strong and white as they had been in youth, and like all people with beautiful teeth he smiled and laughed often, opening his mouth rather wider than those poor wretches conscious of the gold and silver in their jaws.

The three young people who had traveled a hundred miles to see him sat in a mute row on the porch settle—a girl, and two boys wearing glasses. All their hair was trimmed to the same length, and they were so new from the classroom that they seemed still to be in it. The girl had a little notebook open on her knee.

"After all, we each 'live by an invisible sun within us' and at nineteen this sun is only rising."

The older of the young men just managed not to raise his hand. "Sir, isn't that from *Urn Burial?* 'The invisible sun,' I mean?"

"Yes, you have read it?" August looked surprised. "Good. Very good."

The young man's ears reddened with pleasure, and the girl wrote in her notebook: "Urn Burial. Who by?" It would hardly do to ask.

"Was this before or after you had written *Gravehollow*, Mr. Hammer?" said the boy, made bold by his success. "The Thomas Browne title made me think of yours. I believe that *was* your first novel, wasn't it?"

"Thos. Brown. Look up," wrote the girl.

"I had just completed it," August said. "That was another reason for my roosterness. A novel written and accepted by a publishing house, and I was nineteen years old. Nineteen!" he said, laughing again and shaking his massive head, as if the age of nineteen was a rather foolish affliction to be visited on one. He got up from his chair and started pacing to and fro. His figure was excellent; he had a flat stomach, broad shoulders, and a deep broad chest. The three young people, motionless and attentive, waited for him to speak again; compared to him they had the meager half-finished look of turkey poults, and August's wife, Margaret, got up to ring for tea.

"*Gravehollow!* It is a young man's title," August said, pacing. "Who believes in graves and hollows at nineteen? They are far away and all for other people, and since that is the case they may be considered romantic. And yet . . ." He paused for a moment and stood before the screen looking out, through vines, at the far fields. "*Gravehollow* had something. A freshness, I suppose, a morning quality. I was reading it aloud to my family not long ago. We were all rather struck by some of the insights. . . . I often read to them from my work when they are at home. They seem to enjoy it. I hope they do."

He looked at his wife, who smiled. She was used to being invisible. The young people to whom she presently served tea murmured thanks and took the proffered cups and food without seeing her at all. They stared transfixed at August, and afterward would not be able to recall what she had looked like; indeed, it would not occur to them to do so.

The girl cleared her throat. "I think you have three children, haven't you, Mr. Hammer?"

He looked at her benignly. "Ah, now a feminine question.

Yes, we have three. Ernest, Claudia, and Joan. Grown, now, of course."

"And are they—I mean, what do they do?"

"Do? Well, let me see. Ernest is our businessman. When he graduated from Harvard three years ago—"

"Magna cum laude," said Margaret.

"Yes. When he graduated from Harvard three years ago he went into an advertising agency. Of all things, I said, a son of mine in the marketplace! But he has done quite well."

"Really very well," said Margaret.

"And Claudia—what would you say Claudia *does,* Margaret?"

"I would say she's a successful wife and mother. If such a thing is possible."

"But, I mean, don't any of them *write?*" said the girl.

"Joan has tried some little poems lately, I believe."

"The *Atlantic* bought two," said Margaret. She turned the teacup in her hands, and smiled. "Also we have five grandchildren."

"Good God, is it five now?" cried August. "Are you sure, Margaret? Really five?"

The young people laughed.

"Five now, with Ernest's second. You know that perfectly well, August." But she laughed, too.

There was a silence. The girl blushed as she drank her tea because of the loud frank sound of her swallowing. The youngest of the young men was trying to formulate a question which would show that he was sensitive, informed, and original.

There was a sudden long tearing noise in the sky. They looked up to see a jet in its horizontal fall across the blue.

"There it goes, dragging its noise behind it like a sledge," said August. "Another machine pouring din from the sky. Another tune for Hecate. This *is* the music of doom and witchcraft, you know. And it is not made by Russia, nor by Asia, nor by the hydrogen bomb, but simply by the machine. By all machines. Silence has been taken out of the world; we have lived to see the death of silence. What was life like before the machines began to sing? How was it for the Greeks, I wonder? Or the Phoenicians?"

"They probably heard plenty of shouting and horsehoofs and wooden wheels clattering," said Margaret.

"In the cities, perhaps, and those are not strictly the noises of machines. But I am thinking of the country. Here *we* are in the country, forty miles from anywhere, yet even *here,*" he said, lowering his voice as if fearing to be overheard, "even here we are not free. Listen." He closed his eyes and raised a finger. "Now, at this very moment in this seclusion, I can count the sounds of one—two—three—four—five—*six* different kinds of machine. Do you hear that tractor seven fields away? Do you hear the electric mower on my neighbor's farm? And that distant swish and swish is the traffic on the turnpike. And now—that grinding of gears, do you hear?—that's a truck on the back road. Many trucks go by. In the sky—well, the jet has gone, of course, but never mind, there is a regular plane up there. There always is; that sound has grown as common as the sound of breath. And these are not all; why even in the house, this minute, I can hear the snore of the refrigerator; I can hear the electric mixer in the kitchen. And this morning the vacuum cleaner—it's quiet now, thank God —but all morning long the vacuum cleaner was lowing and grazing on our carpets, louder than a cow—"

"Well, it's Tuesday," Margaret said. "It only lows and grazes on Tuesdays and Fridays."

"Wait! I count yet another sound," said August triumphantly, his hand still raised. He opened his blue dramatic eyes and whispered the words, "I hear the little ticking of my wrist watch. I must wear the noise of the flying minutes of my life! All must wear it, or at least hear it, for the machine does not leave time alone. No, it alters it! . . . But this is the subject for another lecture—"

"More tea, any of you?" said Margaret.

"And what do you think of the new forest that is growing

in the world?" demanded August, leaning forward and paralyzing the youngest man with his regard.

"Forest, sir?"

"The rooftree forest! The thousands, the millions of naked spindle trees! They look as starved with death as skeletons, but ah, my God, how alive they are! How lustily alive, all nourished on the juice of mediocrity! And how the people love that juice and tap those trees!"

"T.V.?" wrote the girl in her notebook and nudged the boy on her right, but he glanced coldly at the question and gave her a return nudge that showed her she was obvious.

"And from this forest come now multiplicities of noise." August had started pacing again, and now he stopped abruptly. "There, hear? That's a Diesel groaning and stinking its way to Cleveland. And now, since someone has turned on a hose or flushed a toilet, the electric pump has started its own groaning in our cellar. Where on this dwindling earth is there refuge from the utterances of machines? If I go to the Sahara I will hear an airplane and a jeep. If I climb the Alps I will hear an airplane and a snowplow. If I venture to the remotest canyon I will hear an airplane and a Geiger counter!"

"Maybe skin diving is the answer," said Margaret.

"Frivolity is the besetting sin of wives," said August. "You think I am not serious? But I am serious. What happens to us, subjected as we are to the unremitting sounds of metal in motion?" He paused, looking at his reflection in the dining-room window glass, smoothing back his dense white hair, turning to view his face from a three-quarter angle. "I will tell you what happens. We take these sounds for granted as we take the songs of birds for granted, but there is a difference since they are not the sounds of nature, nor even of man; only of man's inventions. *He,* being nothing but a little mortal pulp, has found it necessary to magnify his sense of authority by inventing all these miracles of hardware that can beat sound at its own race, rub out cities, wash clothes, and so on. But each day that we live with the noise of these inventions as the background for our lives we lose a little of our humanity.

Think of that, each day a little!" He turned, resuming his stride. "Soon we begin to make statues that look like machines, and pictures that look like machines or the wrecks of machines, and stories full of senseless violence and mutilation, such as we have seen much of since the debut of the machine. Yes, to be obvious, what would war be without it? Who would fear war?"

"But in the end perhaps it is a machine that will have killed war," Margaret suggested.

"Frivolity you are permitted, Margaret; sentimentality, no," said August. "Silence! That is what the mind feeds on, the talent grows on! Silence and the sounds of nature and of man. (Of man within reason, of course.) Listen," he stopped before his wife. "I can remember my uncle's wheatfield in Thuringia in July. That was silence! It was hot and dry and yellow in that field; the birds had stopped singing, and the crickets had not yet come; there was no wind. All I could hear was the little crackle of an insect climbing a dry stalk, the tiniest tapping as the full kernels split their husks and dropped. . . . And now and then I could hear the talking voices of my aunt and her daughters, so far away, so gentle! It was not only wheat that was growing in that field. . . .

"*You* young people," he said accusingly, turning toward them. "When have you ever known a stillness like that? You were nursed to the music of radios, rode in cars before your eyes were open, heard ringing telephones and cows of vacuum cleaners as often as you heard your mother's voice! What chance have you? It's not your fault that you have been conditioned like the dogs of Pavlov since the moment you were conceived!"

He stopped abruptly and sat down. A blank, wooden look came into his face. Taking out his pipe he began to pack it with tobacco, and the three watching him saw by the working of his jaws that he was trying to suppress a yawn. They looked at each other uncertainly, stood up. "Sir, we have a long ride ahead of us. . . ."

Now, at the time of leaving, they found their tongues, and

as they left the porch, walking through the house to the front door, they became almost voluble and lingered on the step. . . .

The car that waited for them was obviously the property of someone very young since it was old to the point of eccentricity and painted yellow.

"Another machine to add to the chorus," said the older of the boys, smiling apologetically.

The three of them, ashamed for the moment of being young, settled themselves awkwardly in the front seat. Their heads turned on their turkey-poult necks and they smiled. "Good-by, Mrs. Hammer. Good-by, *sir*. Thank you very, very much!" "Oh, it's been absolutely wonderful!" cried the girl, on a higher note than she had intended. "Memorable!" agreed the youngest man. "Memorable!" he said again, warmly.

The car started up, gave two rude pops from the exhaust, trembled frantically, and plunged forward. The young people waved, and August waved back with his pipe, smiling as if at a little joke. When they were out of sight he sighed and put his hand on Margaret's shoulder.

"Rather touching," he said. "But not remarkable."

"Their appetites were remarkable, anyway. The cake's gone." Margaret stooped to lift a twig from the path. "August, shall we strew the floor with rushes and throw away the vacuum cleaner? Shall we disconnect the phone and hire a foot runner?"

"Foolishness. One has to talk of something. *They* cannot talk."

"I don't think you made them very happy."

"They are young. Must they be happy, too?"

As he walked up the path and opened the screen door he was humming the rondo from *Eine Kleine Nachtmusik*.

His wife chose to stay outdoors, returning slowly to the back of the house. She picked a sprig of mint from the cluster that grew by the porch steps, and stood there smelling it absently and looking out over the curved fields. Another plane was droning softly in the sky; far away, going far away; and upstairs in August's study the typewriter began its tapping.

Apple
Seed
and
Apple
Thorn

October sunshine bathed the park with such a melting light that it had the dimmed impressive look of a landscape by an old master. Leaves, one, two at a time, sidled down through the windless air. High up, the treetops were perfectly still, but down below, on the walks and grassplots, all was a Saturday turmoil of barking dogs and ringing bells and shrieking children.

Barbara and Dickie, still new to the park, entered the playground tentatively. Everyone looked so well established, as if they needed no new friends. On the sunniest benches the mothers sat in a row surrounded by their possessions: baby carriages, toys, sand pails, market bags. They smoked, laughed, talked, yelled admonishment, paused to kiss the wounded. Here and there, since it was Saturday morning, a male parent wandered self-consciously beside a small child or sat and sunned his bald spot as he waited.

"What would you like to do, dear, swing?" suggested Barbara to her son. But Dickie did not hear. Used to country quiet he stood amazed and engrossed, pail in one hand, shovel in the other, staring at the scene before him. The place was a hive of activity. The sandpit seethed with infant life; the seesaws cawed and clanked; the swings flew.

The boys on tricycles made Barbara think of little centaurs, mechanized baby centaurs. There was something so lordly about their progress and their pauses. Magnificent in cowboy

hats, heavily armed with gemmed weapons, they would suddenly convene in a group for as much as a minute at a time,
boasting and vying, still in the saddle, and then at a signal or
an impulse, off they all wheeled together, their fat legs jigging
above the pedals and their cap pistols snapping like popcorn.
Yes, lordly; Dickie found them so. He stood beside her, quietly
staring, too young to use pride as a mask, or to know that it
was ever used for this. He seemed very still and humble at
her side.

"Maybe Dickie will get a bike, too," Barbara suddenly said,
although he had not asked for one.

"Maybe?" he said, and turned his face up to look at her,
smiling his slow perfect smile.

She put her hand under his chin. That's how it begins, she
thought. Mothers begin it. What they've got you shall have,
too, they say; you're just as good as they are, honey, and I'll
teach you to compete first thing.

Dickie gave one little jump, both feet together. "Maybe I
get a bike?" he cried. "A really *bike?*"

"Probably not till Christmastime, my darling."

But Christmas was not a date to Dickie, it was a condition
in which he would find the world one morning on awaking.
There would be a pine-tree smell and all things would have
come true. Who knew when it would happen? It might be
tomorrow.

"I'm going to have a bike, too!" he shouted to a passing
centaur, who responded with a stony glance and continued on
his way.

"Watch out, sonny," warned a man of four, narrowly missing Dickie's toes as he rode by. Dickie shouted the news about
the bike to his departing back.

"*Now* I swing," he said jubilantly, and thrust the pail and
shovel into Barbara's hands.

At the swings she stood in front of him to push so that she
could watch his face as it flew away and then came blooming
toward her, alert and joyful. The reiterative motion, the
occupation, brought to her mind an old count-out chant she

had not thought of in thirty years, and as she pushed her son she said it aloud, making it fit the rhythm of the swing:

> Intery, mintery, cutery, corn,
> Apple seed and apple thorn;
> Wire, briar, limber-lock,
> Three geese in a flock.
> One flew east and one flew west,
> And one flew over the cuckoo's nest.

The rhyme pleased Dickie, and Barbara sang it to him several times, making up a tune to match it. She felt contented, deeply satisfied, without a worry. The past and the future lay asleep like beasts in cages.

A voice beside them burst the spell. "You *dumb,* whaddaya wanna *do,* break open your head?" Barbara turned to see a baby who had tried to stand up in the next swing being slapped into place by the raw red hand of his big stout mother. "My God, whadda I do. Turn my head, just, and here you are half outa the damn swing. You coulda broke your head open!" The scolding went on and on, loud and angry, and during it the rough hand continued to push the swing steadily, reached up to adjust a cap string, reached down to twitch a trouser cuff, busily caring for the baby as the voice railed. He sat impassive, staring at his mother, clad from top to toe in woolen garments though the day was mild. Under the ribbed edge of his cap his dark eyes were trimmed with lashes one inch long. His olive cheeks were smooth and fat, his lips red; he seemed well nourished on his diet of love and fury.

Roused from her trance Barbara turned to look at the neighbors on her left: a woman and a little girl.

"Higher," the child was saying. *"Higher.* I said higher." Her face was expressionless, without color; her hair hung limp into her collar. It was strange that anyone so young and pale could give such an impression of desperation.

Her mother was smiling determinedly and speaking through the smile. "No, you don't need to go any higher. My arms are tired. It's time to go home anyway."

"I said higher," repeated the little girl tonelessly. "Damn you, I *told* you."

"So that's the way you're going to talk, is it?" said her mother with a sort of pleasure, as though some goal had been reached. "Very well, then; swing yourself." She turned and started from the enclosure. Her child, watching her, gave a high wild scream.

"Yes, scream," agreed her mother in a low trembling voice, turning back for an instant. "Go on and scream." Then she walked away, out past the railings and past the slides, red in the face but still smiling, toward the other mothers on the benches.

"But I can't get down by myself," shrieked the little girl. To and fro in lessening arcs she swung and screamed. Tears flashed from her cheeks.

"I'll help you down," Barbara offered.

"No, no. I want my mommy to."

"I guess she wants her mama to," the mother of the wool-clad baby translated helpfully.

The little girl's swing came to a stop. She sat in it, a captive, her feet in black-strapped slippers dangling, her face expressionless again, with tear tracks drying on her cheeks. She sat there for a long time.

"Would you like a push?" Barbara offered at last.

"No," said the child remotely.

The mother returned.

"Now are you ready to go home?"

"No. You push me. Push me high."

"Oh, Estelle! Please let's go *home*."

"You push me."

"Just once more then, understand? This time I mean it."

It was plain to see who was the victor, if such an outcome could be called a victory. The mother, her face sad and raddled with resentment, regarded her daughter without joy, and the child stared back, expressionless; a pair of enemies faced one another.

Barbara stopped Dickie in mid-air to press a kiss on his

warm cheek. Life is so dangerous, she thought; people are so dangerous for each other. Love is so spotty.

Everywhere were signs of rage. In the swarming sand pit they were constantly on view. Often as not the shovel was brought down upon a head; often as not the dimpled hand reached out to slap; and sand, a loose and handy weapon, was forever being hurled to sting the foe.

Now, as though her thoughts had been a prelude, she became aware of a commotion near the slides and turned to see two adults, two fathers, engaging in an argument. Their voices were suddenly rising, transcending the prosaic bounds of ordinary conversation.

One man she recognized, a European, small and dark and decent; the other she had never seen before, tall and heavy-set, with his wife beside him and two scared children clinging to his coat.

"Not my child," the little man was saying. "I do not permit anyone to lay a finger on my child! I do the disciplining!"

"Do it, then! Your kid comes up the ladder behind my kid and pushes him, a big push—"

"It was an accident, I tell you. He did not mean it."

"Accident, hell! He done it on purpose! I seen him, my wife seen him, and no kid's going to get away with that with my kid."

"Nevertheless, they are children only. You had no right to slap my son!"

"I'd do it again—"

"You would have me to contend with, or the police!"

The little man was crimson with anger; the big one chalky pale for the same reason. They seemed to tremble toward each other, closer and closer.

"You don't know what the hell you're talkin' about."

"On the contrary, I know *exactly* . . ."

The big woman at Barbara's right left her lump of wool and smiling broadly walked over to the rail of the enclosure and rested her arms on it, openly drinking in the scene. The woman at the left stopped arguing to listen. As for Barbara, though she frowned in distress, was it distress she felt or was it really pleasure? And she was listening as eagerly as any.

Then suddenly it was over. The big man, muttering, was stalking from the playground, his family hurrying beside him. The little foreigner, no longer crimson, seated himself on a bench and opened a newspaper that quivered in his hands. Outrage had fatigued him, but for the onlookers the air had been mysteriously cleared.

"I thought the little fella was goina hit the big fella," the baby's mother said to Barbara, happy and hearty. "Gee, I thought sure he was goina knock'm down. Come on, Joe, we gotta go home and eat." Loving, maternal, she unloaded her baby from the swing, while at the left, the little girl made no further objection when her mother lifted the bar; also refreshed, it seemed, she slipped down and skipped from the enclosure.

Now, as people departed and noise diminished, a stuttering sound of machinery came from across the park.

"Look, Dickie," said Barbara, stopping the swing. "I see a steam roller over there."

"A steam roller!" Dickie was down in an instant and on his way, his red overalls flashing and his mother jogtrotting in his wake along the concrete pathway to the far side of the park.

The roller, a squat orange machine, backed and bunted fussily on its carpet of wet tar. In its saddle sat the driver, lordly as any tricycle rider and lordly in exactly the same way. An audience admired him.

Nearby on the grass a bench had been constructed with a board and two saw horses. Some workmen sat there with their lunch pails, a yellow-leafed bush spread out beyond them like a fan. One was drinking wine from a bottle wrapped in newspaper; one was slicing an onion onto some bread; the one on the end, finished with his meal, sat idle, his hands clasped loosely between his knees. He had stuck a pink paper carnation into his cap. The shoes, clothes, caps of all of them were dim and work-colored; their faces seemed relaxed and blank.

In their short hour of repose they might have been the laborers of any century; Brueghel had painted many like them.

The one with the carnation turned his head and looked at Dickie standing near. He held out his big shovel of a hand. Dickie inspected it warily and backed away, his own hands clasped behind him.

The man laughed and glanced at Barbara. He had white teeth and two broad disarming dimples. His eyes seemed more mobile than other people's eyes; they rolled in his face like dark marbles. His expression was simple and benevolent and gay. Presently he turned away and spoke to his companions.

Dickie waited a moment or two and began cautiously to advance, paused, and seeing that nobody was going to coax him, climbed up on the end of the board bench and perched beside the man. Sudden pleasure and triumph were in the laborer's face; his great hand pulled Dickie close and then traveled up to stroke the little boy's cheek with a finger tough as kindling wood. From where she stood Barbara could hear the deep, masculine tones of his voice, then Dickie's piping treble in reply. She liked what she saw: the Brueghel men, the golden bush, the paper flower, the friendship formed without a bond. After a while it was with reluctance that she approached.

"Come, Dickie, it is time for lunch."

"No." He frowned at her. "I like it here."

"But I'm afraid we must go."

"No. I don't want to."

The shovel hand pressed Dickie's shoulder and released it.

"Yes, yes," said the man. "You gotta do lika Mama says. Gotta go home, gotta eat, get strong to fighta da big guys, see? Gotta *fight,* see?" And smiling gently he bowed out his elbows and made his mighty hands into two fists.

Dickie accepted his advice and slipped down, walking backward to his mother, still watching his new friend with admiration. Halfway across the park he continued to turn and wave farewell.

Suddenly the sun was gone. Gray clouds had taken up the sky and a few large separated drops of rain drove the last of the loiterers out of the playgrounds. All at once the park seemed darkened and desolate, the falling leaves as sad as rags.

Impervious to the weather, a fat old man in a billowing overcoat approached. He looked like a broken-down sofa with sagging springs and ripped upholstery, covered all over with the keepsakes of past meals. In one hand he carried a paper bag; with the other he sowed the earth with scraps of bread, and down from the air above him came the pigeons. They covered the pavement around him in a piebald mussy crowd. Here were the symbols of peace, waddling and gobbling in the dirt.

Where was that for which they stood, Barbara wondered. Where could she ever find it? Not in herself, alas, nor in anyone she knew or had ever known. Perhaps it did not exist except in the imagination.

Yet even if only in the imagination . . .

"Go! Go! Fly!" cried Dickie, suddenly wild, galloping forward amongst the flock of pigeons and clapping his hands. The sound of their alarmed flight, heavy and cluttered, was like the flapping pages of telephone books. A few feathers fell, a few crumbs, and the old man in the overcoat glared down at Dickie. "Now, whatcha wanna go and do that for?"

"Come, Dickie," said Barbara, taking his hand in hers. "It's late and cold and raining. We must hurry home."

To
the
Victor

Perdita Warren and her little girl, Sully, walked along the empty country street, each carrying a basket. Above them the elm trees, sentimental, Delsartean, arched their old-fashioned branches. Yellow leaves came flickering down. There was no traffic; five minutes ago a couple of tractors stained malachite green with copper sulphate had gangled by. Nothing else. There was no sound except for the mutter of the tractors, now distant in potato fields, and farther still the breaking of the surf. All the children were in school (Sully, not quite three, was still too young) and all the summer people gone away.

"Look, Mommy, I did find a bug," said Sully, stopping.

"So you did, doll, a cricket," agreed Perdita carelessly. Crickets were no novelty at this season; they started from every blade and crevice, sharp as exclamation points. Everything, however, was a novelty to Sully, no cricket just like any other cricket on the earth.

The elms stopped where the sidewalk stopped; beyond, the road curved away to the end of Peyton's Neck, bordered only by the summer people's hedges. The sky, unhindered, was the fiery blue of mid-September.

Perdita sang as she walked. She was wearing shorts, an old sweater, flat sandals; her smooth hair was held at the temple with a barrette. In her dress, at least, she looked younger than Sully, who was buttoned into a rather grandmotherly pinafore with shoulder ruffles and whose hair was strained severely from her forehead with a round comb. Sully walked nicely, a child's walk, with her toes pointing straight ahead and her stomach sticking out.

Beyond the hedges and graveled drives some of the houses were boarded up; all were empty. A few of the summer people would straggle back for weekends till the cold set in, but this was Wednesday, nobody was home.

Ah, how different it was when they were gone! As though many doors had been opened, many veils removed from the sun. From June fifteenth till after Labor Day they, with their weekend husbands, their handsome children, their good-looking cars, took the place by storm; they really believed it to be theirs, never guessing that they themselves, to those who lived there all year round, were a seasonal phenomenon like hybrid corn or Asiatic beetles.

All through the summer mornings those women lay on the beach dozing and gabbling, gabbling of everything under the sun—child-care, beauty-care, garden-care, dog-care; of husbands and politics and the menopause and each other. In the sea they swam, or rather drifted, in batches, still gabbling. And still gabbling, as summer ended, off they all flew at the same time just as the swallows were doing overhead, leaving behind whole fires of zinnias and dahlias in bloom, whole vegetable gardens in which the second crop of lima beans was just beginning to fill out and the squashes were still young and dove-shaped under their green canopies and pipes.

"Let's see; where shall we start?" said Perdita. "Not at the Pembers'; they never leave anything but petunias. And not at the Delaney mausoleum. (Salvia, imagine, and castor beans!)"

Ugly as a horned toad the Delaneys' house glowered behind a prison-guard of spruces. Its shingles were stained brown with creosote and it breathed a faint stink of creosote into the sea air. The Delaneys were old; their tastes had been formed so long ago that they had set, also, at the wrong period.

"God knows what the furniture is like," Perdita said to

Sully. "Golden oak, no doubt, and painted metal bedsteads; everything clean as a pin and awful."

Across the driveway entrance an iron chain was hung like a mayor's necklace, its locket a sign to threaten trespassers.

" 'Keep out!' I bet they have that on their coat of arms," said Perdita bitterly. She thought of Mr. Delaney—bald pate, liver spots, high paunch, large white shoes. Mrs. Delaney—halibut eye and displaced bosom, mouth shaped like a stitch, tiny white shoes.

"He probably speaks of her as 'Mrs. Delaney' even to his friends," she said. "Not that I'd know, of course; he doesn't speak to me. I'm just a Native. So are you."

A Native, quaint and regional, that's the way they thought of her, no doubt. Poor Mrs. William Warren, that young widow who sews (quite nicely, by the way) to make ends meet, and who, though she is a Native and can't afford the dues, is allowed, anyhow, to bring her child to the beach club in the afternoons. Not the mornings, naturally. Poor Mrs. William Warren had for this reason come to know a lot about their children; a lot about the nurses who took care of them, too: the neurotic maternal type, the old burden-carrying type, the wretch who hates children and is paid to punish them by mothers who also, secretly and politely, hate them.

"Pretending to be mothers, pretending to be wives!" exclaimed Perdita. Ah, how she loved despising them!

Sully smiled at her. "Betend?" she said. "Betend I be a mummy?"

"No, honey, you're going to be a real one, just like me. And a real wife, too, who works to please a man."

Oh, but the lovely day, the sparkling air! Anger simply melted in it, even Perdita's durable and cherished anger; suddenly she tossed her basket in the air and caught it. Sully immediately tossed hers too, and dropped it. When she bent over, her whole little heart-shaped bottom in white-cotton pants was presented to view.

"And think of the presents they don't know they give us,"

Perdita said. "Flowers and fruit and beets and carrots and peeks into their windows, even."

They came to a bank of untrimmed privet, high and raggedy, then to a driveway full of weeds.

"Let's see what Miss Chalmers has left for us," said Perdita, turning in. This old woman was a friend of hers. It was said of her that she was rich enough to be eccentric, but the truth was that she would have been completely herself, therefore eccentric, in any walk of life. Her house was painted a strong ugly blue which she spoke of fondly as a "Mediterranean color." When her hollyhocks stopped blooming she made new flowers out of crepe paper and stuck them onto the stalks with Scotch tape. All cats were her friends; no dogs. She drove a twenty-seven-year-old Packard and wore an ash-blond wig above her plum-colored face. (Everybody knew she drank.)

A galaxy of Scarlett O'Hara morning-glories glared at Perdita and Sully from the woodshed wall. The grass, unmowed for weeks, was full of cat's food dishes and the backbones of fish. The garden, as rich in weeds as flowers, still bloomed lustily; huge dahlias fell forward on their stems from weight alone, and the marigolds were five feet high, studded all over with blossoms as hard as doorknobs. Everything was orange or purple or vermilion; you would never find sweet peas or mignonette in Miss Chalmers' gardens; you would never find a tender current in her character. Each summer she adored her crop of cats and pampered them, but every autumn on the day before she returned to the city she drove them all to Dr. Breck's and had them put to death.

"I wonder why I like her so much," Perdita said to Sully, who had found a gin bottle and three cat dishes and was playing house on the kitchen doorstep. "People who do exactly what they want in spite of everybody never should be likable."

Still, Miss Chalmers on her ruthless course was honest; she openly demanded and if firmly refused would not resent. In this she was different from Nina Kimberley. Nina was the one who had stopped her Cadillac convertible in front of Perdita's small house one day and come up the pathway smiling, looking favored and lovely. Perdita on the porch had risen gladly, thinking, Maybe work? Maybe a friend? Until she found out that what Nina wanted was the Adam mantel she had heard that Perdita had in her living room.

"I'd be so glad to pay you anything you ask. . . ."

Perdita had since thought of many a suitable reply to the request, but none at the time. No, at the time she had just gone on smiling and saying, No, she couldn't; No, honestly she couldn't; the house had belonged to her great-grandmother, the mantel, too, and really she just couldn't. . . .

Perdita had never been worth a smile to Nina Kimberley after that, and whenever Nina had sewing to be done she drove to Leighton and gave it to Gertrude Rowls, who had no more style sense than a pelican. If by chance the two young women met in the village streets or shops Nina's blue-crystal eyes looked through Perdita dreamily as if she had vanished from her consideration; perhaps she really had. On the other hand Nina did not disappear for Perdita: visually she was intensified; resentment intensified her. Through the heat-shimmer of this resentment Nina glittered for her with a persistence which was the opposite of infatuation, though as false and magical as infatuation.

In reality she was a very pretty, spoiled young woman with a perfect figure, golden hair, an armful of clashing bracelets. She had three little pruned poodles, though just one child: a stout unhappy girl of six named Tabitha, who was cared for by someone they called Nanny. Though she came from Arkansas and was named Helen Edna McIlvaine, still they called her Nanny. . . . On weekends one glimpsed Nina's husband at her side, tall and somber like a late-afternoon shadow. He looked no happier than Tabitha, Perdita thought, but perhaps no one close to Nina looked really happy except the poodles.

"Bitch!" exclaimed Perdita, snapping off nasturtiums with her fingernails.

"Bits?" echoed Sully sweetly, looking up from her peculiar tea set.

Perdita laughed aloud. Soon she would have to temper her language to Sully's growing comprehension. Already Perdita said too much to her, used her too much.

"Oh, I need a man to talk to!" she said, groaning even as she laughed.

There were male ears at her disposal: those of Ernest Roper, a dentist; of Earle Fondee, a bachelor in the declining forties who kept fresh flowers before his mother's picture. There was no one else. She could not afford to travel, and was already thirty-three.

"Come, Sully, let's get going."

The Farraday house was the next stop, sparkling on its bosom of green lawn. The Farradays, industrious as wasps, were always working at their place—painting the pickets, clipping the hedges, moving the sprinkler lovingly, as if it were a helpless invalid, from place to place. Their married children, their weekend guests, all were put to work when they came to stay.

"It's nice they're so conscientious," said Perdita approvingly. "Just look at these tomatoes! Eat one, Sully. Beets, too. I'll make some borscht tonight."

Happily in the strong sunlight they gleaned their harvest. Sully picked the huge fringed petunias right off at their necks, and bit into seven different apples. She found a plastic clothespin and a penny, and one leftover yellow rose that smelled of pekoe tea.

Beyond the Farraday house was the imposing Allbright house, but the gardener there was such a watchdog that they passed it by. Then came the Converse cottage, exactly like the house on a greeting card: pink window boxes, trellis over the door, heart-shaped apertures in the shutters. One did not need to spy to know that the floors inside would be neatly stamped with small hooked rugs, the walls adorned with Godey prints. Amid this daintiness the big, bluff Converses and their boys lived like a family of trained bears.

Their flowers were what you might expect; all the dahlias were pink or white, the morning-glories heaven-blue. "But no one can sentimentalize an onion, thank goodness," said Perdita as she kicked up a few in the vegetable garden. The cabbages, too, were realistic, bold-smelling, standing firmly, the last of the sulphur butterflies dancing above them. Perdita picked one for the borscht. Sully prowled amongst the house shrubbery getting sticks in her hair and cobwebs in her lashes, but she was not unrewarded: under the rainspout there was an emerald pincushion of moss; beside the kitchen steps many bottle caps and a Yo-yo.

"Sully where *are* you? Come on out, doll. It's getting late, and my basket's heavy, is yours? We'll just stop at the Kimberleys' and then go home."

Ah, admit that this house has been the goal since the beginning! Admit to anger and excitement as it comes into view, gleaming among its tufts of silver willow!

They entered the gates to a fanfare of noon whistles: from Leighton, Wallport, and New Cambridge. The sun itself was shouting midday from the sky.

In Nina Kimberley's garden the scabiosa flowers were dark as garnet brooches, the nicotiana a veil of tossing crimson stars. Nothing was usual, or a dull color. All was exceptional, designed to be exceptional since it had been planned as the background for a beauty *by* the beauty.

"Look, Mommy, there's a swing! Come and push me!"

Perdita hesitated, wavered. "Well, okay, for just a minute." She felt queerly exhilarated, a little dizzy from too much sunshine. As she pushed the swing she began to sing in a loud voice: " '*Sail* bonny boat like a *bird* on the wing *over* the sea to Skye. . . .' " Her child swung up out of the shadow into cerulean light, back into shadow and up again. The bangs on her brow stood up and collapsed, stood up and collapsed; the shoulder ruffles of her pinafore fluttered like wings; her toes, bare and grass stained, were pointed straight before her. She laughed as she flew, and her mother laughed with her, still shouting the song.

" 'Carry the *lad* that was born to be' . . . Oh dear!" Sully was caught jarringly in mid-flight; her head wobbled.

"Ow, Mommy," she protested, but her mother, above her head, was speaking to someone else, a tall man who had come out of the house.

"Oh, Mr. Kimberley," she was saying in the unreal, laughing voice that grownups often use to each other, the voice that makes a child feel lonesome, "it *is* Mr. Kimberley, isn't it? Will you ever forgive us? *Can* you forgive us? You've caught us redhanded. We thought you'd all gone back to the city, so we came plundering and looting." One hand held Sully close as though to silence her, the other gestured to the baskets on the grass, spilling out their treasure. "Sully and I turn into pirates every fall," she added.

"Very attractive pirates," said the man gallantly. "A pair of September buccaneers." He seemed pleased with this phrase and repeated the last two words of it, laughing appreciatively. Perdita laughed too. Sully stared like an owl.

"Officially we have gone," he said. "But I came back alone because I had a job of thinking to do, a decision to make, and I had an idea that this would be a good time and place to get them done in. It hasn't worked out like that, though. I'm getting nowhere."

"Oh, nobody should ever try to come to a decision while living near the sea," Perdita agreed. "It never seems to let you alone. It keeps on interrupting and insisting." She considered this remark nonsense but hoped it was the sort of thing that would impress him.

"That's absolutely right; that's very astute!" he cried admiringly. She had not guessed his face would be so genial. Hitherto he had been a man in profile only; a handsome, peevish profile flying past with Nina in the Cadillac on summer afternoons or staring seaward from the beach. Now, turned to her, his face was friendly—rather soft from granted wishes, rather vain, but friendly and not insensitive.

"I'm not quite certain—I mean I don't think we've met before, have we?"

"I'm Perdita Warren. The Village Seamstress."

That startled him. "Of course you're kidding."

"No, word of honor, it's the truth."

"But you don't seem at all the *type,* I mean."

"I know, isn't it queer? I've even had a college education."
But that was not the tone to take. Pride must be wisely hus-
banded, not spent on trifles. She smiled quickly. "I like my
work very much and the summer people are so darling to us
both."

"Both? Only two?"

"Yes, I'm a widow." Before he could offer the uncomfortable
sympathy of a stranger she hurried on. "We really manage
very well. Sully—this is my daughter Mary Sullivan Warren,
by the way—is a wonderful companion, and we have our own
house that we love; the small gray one on the corner of Sea
Road, you know?"

"The saltbox? It's a little gem!"

"Yes, and unspoiled, too, luckily. It's been in the family
forever and hardly anything's been changed. If my great-
grandmother returned to life I think she'd be able to find her
way about the house in the dark. Of course the plumbing
might surprise her."

"I'd love to see it. Couldn't I drive you back and come in
for a moment? Or I know! You stay here for lunch with me
and *then* I'll drive you back."

Perdita smiled at him over the respectable barrier of her
child's head. Her dishevelment became her and she knew it.
The tension and envy that in summer shrank her face a little
had vanished from her features, and she knew this, too.

"I'm awfully sorry." Slowly she smoothed down Sully's bangs
with one finger. "This place is like all other little places, I
suppose. Petty, you know. Gossipy, with a set of stiff, old-
fashioned rules. In this town women just don't lunch in the
houses of married gentlemen whose wives are absent. So I'm
afraid we really mustn't stay. I wish we could."

Again he was astounded. "But, good heavens, we're chap-
eroned! I mean, look, I mean your little girl . . ."

"Even so. I know it's silly."

There was a heavy silence before he spoke again. "Well,

you know the mores of the place. If you live in it I suppose you must conform."

He was really disappointed; she could feel it. He must detest his exile; to whom was he boasting he could bear it?

"But on the other hand, I don't see why it wouldn't be all right for you to have a meal with *us*," she said. "With Sully and me. For some reason the rules permit this now and then. Come tonight, why not? Come to supper, and then you can see the house."

"But it would be a nuisance for you to have to cook."

"Nuisance? Why, I always cook." She laughed at him. "I can't afford anyone to do it for me!"

"Oh, it's not that. I didn't mean that." He was embarrassed and awkward, as though not to be able to afford a cook was to be handicapped in some way, and it had been tactless, dreadful of him, to have alluded to it. She let him flounder for a second, then rescued him again.

"But I honestly love to cook, and tonight I'm going to make a thief's borscht from all this plunder. It's really good, and I want someone to admire it. Do please come!"

"Of course I will. Of course I meant to from the first." He laughed and fell silent, still smiling and staring at her—too long a stare, a look from which it became difficult to disengage himself.

Perdita basked in its light and thought of the evening ahead. She had on her living-room wall a Winslow Homer water color that had been her aunt's. She had the lacy Adam mantel that Nina had desired. She had her grandmother's old square piano which, though it yielded nothing but irritable pangs of sound, was made of rosewood, elegantly shaped. . . . The dark comes early on September nights; Sully would go to bed right after supper. Perdita would light the lamps, perhaps the fire, and then if he liked music she would put the Archduke records on the old Victrola. She had many a surprise in store for him.

"Mommy let's *go*," demanded Sully, bored to the breaking point and hungry.

"All right, doll. So then it's settled, isn't it, Mr. Kimberley? Can you come early? About six? Because of Sully, you know."

His glance at Sully was perhaps a little bleak. Evidently small children did not figure in his idea of festivity. Still, Perdita was not displeased.

He walked with them to the gate where Sully would not say good-by, and stood watching as they walked away. Monarch butterflies speckled the brilliant air. The wind was freshening; it tousled Perdita's smooth hair. In her basket the flowers burned with their pure colors, and on her backbone, warm as the sunshine, she could feel his steady gaze.

The
Signature

The street was wide and sloped
gently upward ahead of me. It was paved with hard-baked
dust almost white in the early-afternoon light, dry as clay
and decked with bits of refuse. On either side the wooden
houses stood blind to the street, all their shutters closed. The
one- and two-story buildings—some of them set back a little;
there was no sidewalk—had door yards with dusted grass and
bushes, but many of them stood flush to the road itself with
nothing but a powdered weed or two for grace. All of the
houses had an old, foreign look, and all were unpainted,
weather-scoured to the same pale color, except for the eaves
of some which had been trimmed with wooden zigzags and
painted long ago, like the crude, faded shutters, in tones of
blue or red.

The sky was blanched with light, fronded with cirrus, un-
emphatic; just such a sky as one finds near the sea, and this,
in addition to the scoured, dry, enduring look of the town,
persuaded me that an ocean or harbor must be somewhere
near at hand. But when I came up over the rise of the road,
I could find no furred line of blue at any horizon. All I could
see was the great town—no, it was a city—spread far and
wide, low lying, sun bleached, and unknown to me. And this
was only one more thing that was unknown to me, for not
only was I ignorant of the name of the city, but I was ignorant
of my own name, and of my own life, and nothing that I

seized on could offer me a clue. I looked at my hands: they were the hands of a middle-aged woman, coarsening at the joints, faintly blotched. On the third finger of the left hand there was a golden wedding ring, but who had put it there I could not guess. My body in the dark dress, my dust-chalked shoes were also strangers to me, and I was frightened and felt that I had been frightened for a long time, so long that the feeling had become habitual—something that I could live with, in a pinch, or, more properly, something that until this moment I had felt that I could live with. But now I was in terror of my puzzle.

I had the conviction that if I could once see my own face, I would remember who and what I was, and why I was in this place. I searched for a pane of glass to give me my reflection, but every window was shuttered fast. It was a season of drought, too, and there was not so much as a puddle to look into; in my pocket there was no mirror and my purse contained only a few bills of a currency unknown to me. I took the bills out and looked at them; they were old and used and the blue numerals and characters engraved on them were also of a sort I had never seen before, or could not remember having seen. In the center of each bill, where ordinarily one finds the pictures of a statesman or a monarch, there was instead an angular, spare symbol: a laterally elongated diamond shape with a heavy vertical line drawn through it at the center, rather like an abstraction of the human eye. As I resumed my walking I was aware of an impression that I had seen this symbol recently and often, in other places, and at the very moment I was thinking this I came upon it again, drawn in chalk on the side of a house. After that, watching for it, I saw it several times: marked in the dirt of the road, marked on the shutters, carved on the railing of a fence.

It was this figure, this eye-diamond, which reminded me, by its persistence, that the eye of another person can be a little mirror, and now with a feeling of excitement, of possible hope, I began walking faster, in search of a face.

From time to time I had passed other people, men and

women, in the street. Their dark, anonymous clothes were like the clothes of Italian peasants, but the language they spoke was not Italian, nor did it resemble any language I had ever heard, and many of their faces had a fair Northern color. I noticed when I met these people that the answering looks they gave me, while attentive, were neither inimical nor friendly. They looked at me with that certain privilege shared by kings and children, as if they possessed the right to judge, while being ignorant of, or exempt from, accepting judgment in return. There is no answer to this look and appeal is difficult, for one is already in a defensive position. Still, I had tried to appeal to them; several times I had addressed the passers-by hoping that one of them might understand me and tell me where I was, but no one could or would. They shook their heads or lifted their empty hands, and while they did not appear hostile, neither did they smile in answer to my pleading smiles. After they had passed I thought it strange that I never heard a whisper or a laugh or any added animation in their talk. It was apparently a matter of complete indifference to them that they had been approached in the street by a stranger speaking a strange language.

Knowing these things I thought that it might be difficult to accomplish my purpose, and indeed this proved to be the case. The next people I met were three women walking together; two were young and one was middle-aged. I approached the taller of the young women, for her eyes were on a level with my own, and looking steadily into them and coming close, I spoke to her.

"Can you tell me where I am?" I said to her. "Can you understand what I am saying?"

The words were a device, I expected no answer and got none of any sort. As I drew close she looked down at the ground; she would not meet my gaze. A little smile moved the corners of her lips, and she stepped aside. When I turned to her companions they also looked away, smiling. This expression on other faces might have been called embarrassment, but not on theirs. The smile they shared seemed noncommittal, secretive, knowledgeable in a way that I could not fathom, and afterward I thought it curious that they had shown no surprise.

For a long time after that I met no one at all. I met no cat, no dog, no cabbage butterfly; not even an ant on the packed, bald dust of the road, and finally rejecting its ugliness and light I turned to the left along another street, narrower and as graceless, and walked by the same monotony of weather-beaten houses. After a few minutes I heard a sound that halted me and I stood listening. Somewhere not far away I heard children's voices. Though their words were foreign they spoke also in the common tongue of children everywhere: voices high, eruptive, excited, sparked with the universal jokes, chants, quarrels of play; and here, listening to them, my memory stirred for the first time—a memory of memory, in fact. For whatever it was that nearly illuminated consciousness was not the memory itself, but a remnant of light which glowed on the periphery of the obstacle before it: a penumbra.

Where are the children, I thought; where are they! With great urgency and longing I set out in the direction of their voices, determined to find them and in doing so to find something of myself. Their voices chattered, skipped, squabbled like the voices of sparrows, never far away, but though I turned and hunted and listened and pursued I could not find them. I never found them, and after a while I could not hear them either. The ghostly light of memory faded and was extinguished, and my despair rose up in darkness to take its place.

The next person I met was a man, young and dark-browed, and when I confronted him and asked my questions, it was without hope. I knew he would not meet my look, or let his eyes show me my longed-for, dreaded face. Yet here I was wrong; he stood before me without speaking, but the gaze with which he answered mine was so intense and undeviating that it was I who dropped my eyes and stepped aside. I could not look, and soon I heard him going on his way.

I had been walking a long time, and the light was changing;

the sun was low and full in my face. West, I said to myself;
at least I know west, and I know that I am a woman, and
that that is the sun. When the stars come out I will know
those, too, and perhaps they will tell me something else.

After a while I sat down on a wooden step to rest. I was
struck by the silence of the city around me, and I realized
this was because it was a city of walkers who walked on dust
instead of on pavements. I remembered that I had seen no
mark of a wheel on any road, and that nothing had moved
in the sky all day except for a few birds in flight.

A breath of dry wind crept along the dust at my feet, and,
far away, a noise of knocking started, a sound of stakes being
driven into the ground with a wooden mallet. Desolate, re-
iterated, it sounded as though somewhere in the city they
were preparing a gallows or a barricade. Too tired and
dispirited to move I sat there listening to the double knock-
and-echo of each blow. A few people passed me on their way
home, each of them giving me the glance of casual appraisal
I had seen so often. Doors opened and doors closed, the sun
went down, and soon the street was still again and the knocking stopped. Where would I sleep that night, or find a meal?
I neither knew nor cared.

One by one the stars came out on the deepening sky, perfect, still, as if they were really what they seemed to be—calm
ornaments for hope, promises of stillness and forever.

I looked for Venus, then Polaris, then for Mars. I could not
find them, and as the stars grew in number, coming imper-
ceptibly into their light, I saw with slow-growing shock that
these were not the stars I knew. The messages of this night
sky were written in a language of constellations I had never
seen or dreamed. I stared up at the brand-new Catherine
wheels, insignias, and fiery thorn crowns on the sky, and I do
not think that I was really surprised when I spied at the
zenith, small but bright, a constellation shaped like an elongated diamond, like the glittering abstraction of a human
eye. . . .

It was just at this moment, before I could marshal or

identify my thoughts in the face of such a development, that I heard a sound of trees, wind in the leaves of trees, and I realized, irrelevantly it seemed, that in all my walking in this city—how many hours, how many days?—I had not seen a single tree, and the sound of their presence was as welcome as the sound of rain is after a siege of drought. As I stood up it occurred to me that neither had I seen one child among all the strangers I had met, that though I had heard the children I had not been able to find them, and now to all the other fears was added the fear that the trees, too, would magically elude me.

The street was dark, though light was glimmering through the cracks of the closed shutters. What was left of sunset, green as water, lay on the western horizon. Yet was it really western? In a sky of new stars, was it not possible and in fact probable that what I had believed to be the sun was not really Sun at all? Then what were the compass points, what were the easts and wests of this city? And what would I find when once I found myself?

I heard the beckoning of trees again and as if they were the clue to sanity, I ran along the street in the direction of their sound. I turned a corner, and there, ah yes, there were the trees: a grove of tall, dry, paper-murmuring trees that grew in a little park or public garden where people were walking together or sitting on the dusty grass. At the center of this park or garden there was a great house of stone, the first stone building I had seen all day. It was lighted from top to bottom; the lights of its long windows twittered in gold among the small leaves of the trees, and a door stood open at the head of a flight of steps.

I passed many people on the path, but now I did not look at them or ask them questions. I knew that there was nothing they could do for me. I walked straight to the steps and up them and through the door into the lighted house. It was empty, as I had expected, a great empty ringing house, but there was a splendor about it, even in its emptiness, as if those who had left it—and left it recently—had been creatures of joy, better than people and gayer than gods. But they, whoever they were, had gone. My footsteps sounded on the barren floor, and the talk of the loiterers outside, the foreign talk, came in the windows clearly on the night air.

The mirror was at the end of the hall. I walked toward it with my fists closed, and my heart walked, too, heavily in my chest. I watched the woman's figure in the dark dress and the knees moving forward. When I was close to it, I saw, low in the right-hand corner of the mirror, the scratched small outline of the eye-diamond, a signature, carved on the surface of the glass by whom, and in what cold spirit of raillery? Lifting my head, I looked at my own face. I leaned forward and looked closely at my face, and I remembered everything. I remembered everything. And I knew the name of the city I would never leave, and, alas, I understood the language of its citizens.